In D Marie's first work of Glass Hill, she introduces you to some characters that are easy to love, and some that are harder to love. What a great picture of real life! Throughout the tale, readers are prompted to reflect on the challenge of patience in affliction, the living and active nature of God's Word, and the joy that comes through Christian forgiveness. One of the lovely strengths of this book is its gentle tone that will calm readers from the first page to the last, while also giving plenty of opportunity to think, learn, and grow.

Rosie Adle is a pastor's wife and mom who loves to read aloud to her five children. She is co-author of *LadyLike: Living Biblically*, a collection of thoughtful essays for Christian women.

Journey to the Glass Hill, was a delightful, heart-warming book. I found the characters to be charming and enchanting. This is a true story of love, forgiveness, and reconciliation based upon Biblical principles. As a 4th grade teacher, there is much value in this book being added into the classroom. *Journey to the Glass Hill* is written age appropriately and would hold the attention of 3rd through 5th grade students. I appreciate the author's ability to reach this audience as it can be a struggle to find books with Christian values. The message of God's provision resonates throughout the book. This would be a great book to read aloud to students as well as for them to read on their own. I look forward to being able to share this book with my own children as well as those I teach.

Kathy Maske, 4th Grade Teacher, Good Shepherd Lutheran School, Collinsville, IL

Journey to the Glass Hill

Journey to the Glass Hill

D Marie

Illustrated by
Reverend Brian King

Copyright © 2019 by D Marie

All rights reserved. No part of this book may be used or reproduced by any means, graphic, electronic, or mechanical, including photocopying, recording, taping or by any information storage retrieval system without the written permission of the author except in the case of brief quotations embodied in critical articles and reviews.

Scripture taken from the King James Version of the Bible

This is the work of fiction. All of the characters, names, incidents, organizations, and dialogue in this novel are either the products of the author's imagination or are used fictitiously.

www.DMarieBooks.com

Any people depicted in stock imagery provided by Getty Images are models, and such images are being used for illustrative purposes only.
Certain stock imagery © Getty Images.

ISBN: 978-1-7340520-0-8

Library of Congress Control Number: 2018912118

Printed in the United States of America

Dedication

To my husband for his love and support

Special Acknowledgements

*The Lord, my Provider,
who gave the inspiration for this book*

*Glenda Jameson for her friendship,
prayers, and editing help*

Contents

Introduction

1 The Gift 1

2 The Angel Returns 7

3 Bond of Love 15

4 Trip to Town 19

5 The Announcement 23

6 The Preparations 27

7 The Wedding Gift 33

8 Big Surprise 39

9 New Direction 45

10 New Addition 49

11 Another Addition 55

12 Tragedy Strikes 61

13 Royal Arrival 69

14 A New Home 75

15 Always Remember 81

16 New Life Begins 87

17 The Lord Provides 93

18	The Music Stopped	99
19	New Responsibilities	103
20	The Word is Found	111
21	Honor is Given	115
22	Patience	121
23	The Visitor	129
24	Business is Good	133
25	A Memorable Day	137
26	The Ride	145
27	Important Decision	149
28	The Contest	157
29	Brass	161
30	Silver	169
31	Gold	175
32	The Reunion	179
33	The Revelation	183
34	The Restoration	189

Discussion Starters   195

Acknowledgements   199

About the Author and Artists   201

Introduction

Journey to the Glass Hill is part one of a trilogy. The story begins with two families during the early 1600s in northern Europe. As time goes by, the families expand, and more characters are included. Each one of the characters has an impact on the lives around them. Some of the effects are positive, and some are negative. How the people respond to their situations reflects upon their personal qualities and character traits. The role of the father is evident throughout the trilogy.

The purpose of the trilogy is to offer a Christian-based folktale to model how faith and a personal relationship with the Lord can help overcome the trials of life. Prayers and Scriptures are woven into the story as they are fundamental in the relationship with God.

Discussion starters for the chapters are located at the end of the book.

Enjoy the journey,

D Marie

Chapter 1

The Gift

Long ago in a faraway land, a soft breeze blew on a warm summer evening. The gentle wind ruffled the leaves and swayed the tall grass. It continued its journey over gently rolling hills, through the thick forests, and into the open lands that surrounded the town of Christana where it kissed a nearby winding river, sending ripples across the surface to mark its passing.

Centuries ago, the rulers of this land named it Christana. As time went by, many villages were established throughout the kingdom. One particular village became favored by the monarchs, and they built their palace in that location, changing its name to match that of the country. As Christana prospered, it grew faster and larger than all the other villages and expanded into a town. Its countryside abounded with farms that provided food for the people.

One nightfall, the breeze blew across a dusty lane outside the town of Christana. The clouds parted and allowed moonlight to stream through and illuminate a quaint white cottage with a thatched roof. The moon's rays came to rest on a young woman standing at her bedroom window.

D Marie

Her golden hair glistened in the moonlight, and the illumination accentuated her delicate facial features. Johanna, pronounced Yo-HAHN-nah, stood quietly gazing at the neighboring farm where a young man chopped wood in the near darkness. He momentarily stopped to wipe the sweat from his brow. Turning his head, he glanced in Johanna's direction.

Johanna gasped and ducked back out of sight. *Did he see me?* she wondered. *No, I'm too far away.*

Johanna had often noticed Ari working alone, for she had not seen his father in a long time. *Maybe his father is too weak to come outside*, she thought.

Ari had already lost so much. His mother had passed away when he was a child, and now his father's health had been fading over the last few months. Elias, Ari's father, kept to himself and didn't want anyone coming around. "Busybodies," the grumpy man called them. "Leave me alone," he often snapped at people.

Ari had to do everything to keep the farm functioning and often worked into the night. Not sure what she could do to help, Johanna returned to her bed and prayed. "Food!" she said aloud. Remembering that her mother was downstairs sleeping, she threw her hand over her mouth. "I can take them some prepared food," she whispered.

Journey to the Glass Hill

The next morning, Johanna found her mother sitting at the table in the cooking room. Nearby, a kettle of porridge simmered in the fireplace. With a warm smile, Elina greeted her daughter, "Good morning, Johanna. How was your night?" Elina's soothing voice comforted Johanna, and she edged closer just to bask in that serenity.

Elina had a challenging responsibility of being a father as well as a mother. Johanna's father lost his life after a deadly plague had spread through Christana. Many families had lost a loved one during that time.

Johanna had been a young child when her father died. Fortunately, he had left her and her mother with a home and some coins to provide for their needs. She remembered her mother praying for the strength to comfort her during that time of loss, and the Lord had provided. Her mother truly reflected Christian love.

"My night was wonderful, Mama," replied Johanna. She sat down and shared her prayer about helping Ari and his father.

Elina smiled and agreed, "Food would be a thoughtful gift. Let's get started after we eat."

All morning they worked in the cooking room. Elina made everyday chores fun. Sometimes, when Johanna looked away, her stirring spoon disappeared. "Mama, do you see my spoon?" As Elina looked innocently at the ceiling, Johanna retrieved the missing spoon from the fireplace mantle.

Occasionally, Elina's tie in the back of her outfit became undone, and her apron fell to the floor. "Johanna, you silly girl," Elina would chide teasingly. They both giggled and continued to work.

As they cooked and baked, the amazing aromas of their efforts filled the cooking room. A wooden basket rested on the table waiting to be filled. Elina covered the bowls of roast chicken, savory stew, and cooked vegetables with separate cloths and set them in the basket. Johanna wrapped the bread in another cloth and placed the warm loaf on top of the bowls.

Johanna reached for the handle of the basket. Her mother lovingly placed her hand on top of her daughter's hand. "Place both arms under the basket," Elina said. "This much love requires both arms to hold it."

Johanna stopped and hugged her mother. "I hope I'll someday be a wonderful mother just like you."

"You will," Elina said. "Deep in my heart, I know you will." Elina opened the door and placed the heavy basket in Johanna's arms. As Johanna walked down the lane, tears of joy welled in Elina's eyes. She watched her daughter and reflected, *My sweet Johanna is sharing her love.*

As Johanna walked closer to Ari's farm, she heard the cows mooing, the chickens clucking, and the dog barking. Johanna couldn't see Ari's house from her cottage, because his barn was in the way. But as she turned in the lane, his house came into view.

The nearby cottages paled in comparison to this home. Meticulously laid stones comprised the exterior of the large house. His home had a tiled roof instead of the common material of thatch. The barn was also built with stones, but it had a thatched roof. A stone and wooden fence surrounded the entire farm.

No one knew the farm's origin except Elias, and he kept it to himself. His suspicious nature thwarted him from talking with his neighbors. He minded his own business and expected others to do the same.

As she continued her walk, a voice joined the animal sounds, "Hello, may I help you?"

Startled, Johanna whirled around just as Ari stepped out from behind a tree. Their eyes met. For a few moments, they just looked at each other. His kind eyes and warm smile quickly put Johanna at ease. Ari's curly brown hair framed his face. An air of gentle strength surrounded his tall stature. It had been a

Journey to the Glass Hill

long time since they had seen each other. The farm consumed Ari's time, and he seldom left to go anywhere.

The dog rushed to Ari's side, smelled the food, and jumped toward the basket. Ari caught him just in time.

"You can't blame him," Ari said apologizing for his dog. "It smells so good."

"Forgive me. This is for you and your father," replied Johanna.

"Thank you! Father will be delighted to have a good meal. I'm not a good cook," confessed Ari. "Please come in, Johanna. May I carry that basket for you?"

Johanna gladly passed the heavy basket to Ari.

Once inside, Johanna noticed only a few pieces of furniture in the clean and orderly front room. "The cooking room is this way," Ari said with a cheerful voice. His eyes gleamed as he laid the basket on the table.

"Ari, who are you talking to?" called a rough voice from a different room. "I smell bread. We haven't had bread in a long time. Who's here?"

"An angel of mercy," replied Ari. "She brought us a basketful of food."

"Bring her here," ordered the old man. "I want to see an angel."

Johanna cautiously walked with Ari to his father's room. Thick curtains covered the windows, obstructing the sunlight, but she could see an outline of a bedridden man in front of her. He motioned for Johanna to come closer. The illness had robbed him of his energy. Deep lines and wrinkles covered his face and body as evidence of his hard life working in the open fields. His pale skin added to his declining appearance.

Will he be grumpy with me? Johanna wondered, and she apprehensively entered his room. As she edged closer to his bed, Johanna saw kindness in the elderly man's eyes and reached out to touch his face. "Are you hungry?" she asked. "Ari, could you bring some stew and bread for your father?"

A smile appeared on Ari's face. "Yes," he replied, and he quickly left the room.

Elias also had a smile on his face. He reached for Johanna's hand. "Does my angel have a name?" he inquired.

"Yes—that is, I mean, my name is Johanna, and I live in the cottage not far from here. I see Ari outside sometimes, but I haven't seen you in a long time."

Slowly Elias raised his body forward. "I have not been well. Ari works so hard and so long. He's such a good son. I love him dearly, but I can no longer help him. Maybe he will meet someone like his mother that will be a helpmate for him. She was the love of my life, but she died many years ago." Unnoticed, Ari had returned and stood by the doorway listening. Tears gathered in his eyes. "Do you like my son?" inquired Elias.

Immediately, Ari conspicuously cleared his throat and announced, "Your food is here, and it's still warm."

Johanna heaved a sigh of relief, glad that Elias immediately forgot his question and became more interested in the tray of food. She edged toward the door. "Enjoy your meal, everyone. I need to return home." Johanna waved goodbye and walked out of the room.

Chapter 2

The Angel Returns

Johanna's eyes twinkled as she told her mother about her food delivery. Elina smiled as she listened. She could read her daughter like a book. But Johanna's smile faded. Elina watched as her daughter's eyes drifted downward when she described Elias' condition.

"I knew he was not well, but I didn't know the extent of his illness," said Elina. "Let's make more food for Ari and his father later in the week."

I was hoping you would say that, Johanna said to herself not wanting her mother to notice her eagerness to see Ari again.

The following morning, Johanna repeatedly tapped her fingers on the table after she finished eating. "Mama, waiting to prepare our next food basket is taking forever."

"Johanna, are you wanting to cook or visit our neighbors?" Elina asked with a knowing smile.

Johanna blushed. "I enjoy both."

"I do, too. Let's get to work on our orders for clothes so we have coins to buy the food."

Johanna giggled and then became serious. "We're low on fabric. Shall we go to the weavers today?"

"Yes, I could use a good walk."

The majority of their income came from making clothes. Elina and Johanna made frequent trips to town and carried their supplies home. Elina only bought fabric from weavers in Christana who used the best wools. Being a widow and sole supporter of her daughter, many weavers allowed her to have first choice of their fabrics. Being selective, Elina's keen eyes looked for the tightest weaves and consistent widths of yarn. Johanna gave it the cheek check.

"Johanna," Elina began holding up two bolts of cloth, "which do you prefer?"

The young woman closed her eyes and rubbed the woolen fabrics on her face. One was scratchier than the other. "This one is good," Johanna replied as she looked at her mother and pointed to her choice.

After settling the purchase, Elina and Johanna returned home with the fabric to cut the necessary shapes. Their fingers moved quickly to stitch the pieces together to transform the material into jumpers and skirts for girls and women. Pants for boys and men required less fabric but took about the same amount of time to make. The clothing sold quickly as Elina's seamstress skills were well known. Her seams did not come apart, and she allowed extra material for the various sizes of the consumers.

Johanna walked into the cooking room. The soft glow of the dawn's early rays offered a slight illumination. She poked the remaining ashes in the fireplace. The fire had consumed the wood from the previous night and needed more.

Elina walked in. "Good morning, Johanna. Is today the next 'basket of food' day?"

Johanna's face reddened. "Is it that obvious?"

Elina shook her head as she tried not to laugh. They both got busy and prepared the food. With the loaded basket in her arms, Johanna headed for the door.

As the young woman walked down the lane, she saw Ari saddling his horse. He secured the girth under the horse and walked over to Johanna.

"How is your father today?" Johanna inquired.

"Grumpy. Do you want to come in?"

Johanna paused. She shied away from confrontation, especially with men. A slight pucker of disappointment formed

Journey to the Glass Hill

in the corner of her mouth. Her afternoon visit was not what she had envisioned.

"Perhaps your father needs his rest. I'll come in next time." Handing the basket to Ari, she waited for his response.

"Thank you for the food, Johanna. Please thank your mother for me."

"I'll tell her, and you're welcome, Ari."

Ari looked at the ground trying to think of something to add. His mind went blank. He lifted his head and managed to say, "I'll bring your basket over later."

"Anytime when you are not busy."

"That will be a long wait."

They both chuckled and said their goodbyes. Ari carried the basket into his house and heard his father snoring. He smiled and thought, *It's a good thing Johanna didn't come in.*

The following morning, Johanna noticed the cooking room became too warm, and she opened the front door for a welcomed breeze. "Mama, our basket is here, and it's overflowing with root vegetables and salted meat."

Elina came to investigate. She looked at the basket. Then she noticed an unfamiliar shadow on the side of the cottage. "That looks like a stack of chopped wood over there."

Ari had delivered the wood and food during the night. *I bet he's tired today.* Johanna imagined. *He's such a hard worker, and thoughtful, and kind to his father, and....* Her mother's voice broke her train of thought.

"Johanna, this basket is too heavy. Let's both carry it in."

Elina watched her daughter and noticed how her mind wandered away at times. *Johanna is preoccupied. I wonder who she's thinking about.* Elina smiled and never said a word.

"With all this extra food, we should prepare something special for our neighbors. Maybe a sweet treat," Elina offered.

Johanna's eyes sparkled. "That's a wonderful idea."

The women baked some sweet cakes the following day. Afterward, Johanna walked down the familiar lane with her basket. She paused to watch Ari split wood to replenish his diminished woodpile. He looked up and rushed to meet her.

"Good morning, Ari," she greeted as he came closer. "Thank you for the new supplies. We were running low on wood."

"My pleasure. It's the least I can do."

After a quick visit with Elias, Johanna returned home.

Elina and Johanna made several meals to take to their neighbors. One morning while kneading the bread dough, Johanna dropped some flour. A white cloud floated in the air. "Achoo!" went Johanna. Elina looked up and watched as Johanna reached for her nose and smeared flour on her face.

"Need some help?" Elina asked, trying not to laugh. Johanna tilted her head and scrunched her eyebrows together as an inquiring look spread over her face.

"You may want to look in the mirror before you leave," her mother said with a slight grin. Immediately, the young woman walked into her mother's room. Loud laughter poured through the doorway.

Johanna returned to the cooking room wiping her face. "Mama, what would I do without you?"

Still smiling, Elina winked. "I'll always be there for you."

Johanna returned a smile to her mother. Later in the morning, she loaded the basket with the prepared food. She hummed a tune of one of her favorite hymns as she strolled down the lane carrying the wooden container with both arms.

Journey to the Glass Hill

As Johanna approached the farm, Ari tied the reins of his horse to a rail. When he saw her, he raced to the lane to meet her. As he got closer to Johanna, he remembered that he had been cleaning the horse stalls and chicken coop earlier in the day. It didn't matter. His eyes sparkled when he saw Johanna. She had to be an angel, because her face glowed with kindness.

When Ari reached Johanna, she stopped walking and gazed into his eyes. Unfortunately, the hay, dirt, and animal odors overwhelmed her nose, and she sneezed, almost dropping her basket of food. Ari quickly took it with both arms and laughed.

Johanna put both hands on her hips. "What are you laughing at?"

"Because you are from Earth after all."

Lowering her hands, she cocked an eyebrow. "What do you mean?"

"Well," he began, hesitating only slightly, "I don't think angels sneeze. Therefore, you are from Earth. But, you're still an angel to me."

Satisfied with his response, Johanna smiled and blew her nose with her handkerchief. They walked side by side to Ari's home.

As soon as they entered the house, Elias smelled the aroma of the freshly prepared food. "My angel, please come here," he called. As Johanna entered the room, Elias smiled, but he could not disguise the pain in his eyes or the deep furrows in his forehead. She reached for his hand and listened as he strained his voice to talk. "My heart is full of sorrow."

"Would you like me to pray with you?" she offered.

The look in his eyes changed, and his tensed eyebrow muscles relaxed the furrows as new hope came to him. "Yes, please pray."

Ari stood by and quietly listened as Johanna prayed. "Dear Father in Heaven, Elias is Your child, and he needs You. We ask for You to put Your hand upon him and help him. We put our faith in You and Your will. In Jesus' Name, we pray. Amen."

A softness appeared on Elias' face. "Thank you, Johanna. I know the Lord has shown favor toward me." His body remained weak, but Elias had peace.

Johanna held Elias' frail hand while Ari went to the cooking room. Her thumb slid back and forth across his wrinkled skin. She hummed a familiar hymn until Ari returned with a bowl of food and some bread for his father. Johanna bent over and kissed the elderly man on the forehead.

As Johanna left Elias' room, Ari followed her to the door and asked, "What have I done that you would show so much kindness to me?"

Johanna felt her face warm up as her cheeks turned a soft red. *How can I tell Ari I'm falling in love with him?* Johanna thought of another reply and said, "Ari, God loves you, and He uses His people to show His love."

Ari wasn't quite sure of the true meaning of those words, but he liked the sound of "loves you." He moved closer, but that caused her to sneeze as those odors were once again near her nose. The corners of their mouths turned upward. Laughter followed.

Johanna looked down at her apron and adjusted any wrinkles, trying to recompose herself. After bidding Ari farewell, she walked home wearing an even bigger smile.

Journey to the Glass Hill

Ari returned to his father's room and nonchalantly asked, "Papa, do you like Johanna?"

Elias smiled as he lifted his head and looked at his son. "The real question is, *do you* like Johanna?"

"Yes, Papa," Ari admitted, and he took a deep breath. "What should I do?"

"Son, you will know what to say at the right time. One thing for sure, she cooks better than you." Elias lifted his utensil and took another spoonful of stew.

Chapter 3

Bond of Love

The nutty aroma of porridge filled the cottage as it simmered in the fireplace kettle. Johanna and her mother enjoyed their morning meal until they heard someone pounding on the front door. A baffled stare swept over their eyes then they both rushed to see who was there. To their surprise, Ari stood there with an agonizing look on his face.

"Ari, what has happened?" Johanna asked.

"It's my father," he said, summoning the strength to put his thoughts into words. "He has asked for you, his angel. I think he is dying. Will you come?"

"Of course!"

Johanna and Elina accompanied Ari to his home. As they entered, both Johanna and Elina felt a chill in the air even though it was a warm summer morning. Elina held her daughter's hand as they walked through the house. Being around death always brought back painful memories about her father. Ari led the way to his father's room, and he knelt by his father's head.

"Is my angel here?" moaned the elderly man. His weak eyes stared sightlessly about the room.

"Yes, Papa," Ari replied. "Johanna is here with her mother, Elina."

A faint smile appeared on Elias' lips. Johanna moved closer, leaned over his pillow, and touched his face. "I am here," she assured him.

"Now I can leave this Earth and go to the Lord," Elias announced in a low hoarse voice. "You will not be alone, my son. Johanna is here. I love you, Ari." With those words, the elderly man closed his eyes and breathed his last breath. His tranquil face displayed an assuring smile. He went in peace.

Johanna broke down and cried for Elias. Elina started to move forward to comfort her daughter, but Ari stood up and put his arm around Johanna. They laid their heads on each other's shoulder and wept.

Elina wept, too. When she saw Johanna and Ari together, she knew a bond was being formed that went beyond friendship.

Only four people attended the funeral. Elias wanted it that way—no busybodies. He was buried next to his beloved wife.

Ari's grandfather had chosen the family gravesite area many years ago when the farm was built. A small hill blocked its view from the house and barn. Nearby trees provided shade and cooled the air. Wild flowers grew around the headstones displaying their warm colors of the sun and offered a serene background to soothe the heavy heart.

When Elina and the minister left, Johanna quietly stood by Ari's side. Thoughts of his loss and being alone overwhelmed Ari. He had no more family. He turned toward Johanna and said, "I love you, Johanna. Please promise you will never leave. My soul could not bear it."

"Yes, Ari, I love you with my whole heart," Johanna assured him.

Ari reached for her hand. He had more to say to Johanna, but the sudden tolling of bells cut him off. They looked at each other in stunned amazement. The bells kept ringing and ringing. The church bell rang. The palace bell rang.

Journey to the Glass Hill

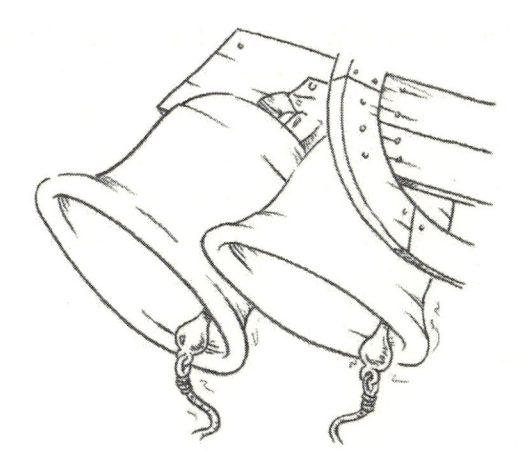

Normally, a ringing bell indicated the time of day, the start of church, or warn of a fire. This unusual pattern of ringing did not communicate any of those conditions.

"What's going on?" asked Ari. "Something is happening in Christana. Let us go see what it is."

Johanna treasured those two words, "let us." It was the first time they were a couple, a team. Ari walked over to the barn and prepared two horses for their ride. Johanna followed him and waited in front of the barn.

Chapter 4

Trip to Town

When Ari came back with the horses, Johanna stiffened and walked backward. Ari saw her reaction. His eyebrows raised in a worried fashion. "What's the matter?"

"I have never ridden a horse," Johanna replied as she looked at the ground.

Ari came closer to Johanna. Tenderly, he put his hand under her chin and lifted her head up. "Johanna, the horse is your friend. If you treat him with love and kindness, he will protect you and take you anywhere you want to go." He gazed into her eyes. "Do you trust me?"

Johanna smiled. "Yes, I do."

"Then come and talk to my horse the same way you talk to me and your mother…the way you talked to my father." Ari gently placed Johanna's hand on the horse's neck.

"You are muscular yet so soft. You are beautiful," Johanna told the horse as her hand glided over his neck.

"Now, look at his eyes," said Ari, "and rub his forehead."

Johanna looked into the horse's eyes and placed her fingers on his forehead and scratched it. The horse lowered his head so Johanna could reach the top of his ears.

"He likes you!" exclaimed Ari. "Why am I not surprised?"

With Ari's encouragement and with the gentleness of the horse, Johanna was ready to try. Ari placed his hands around her waist and lifted her up to the saddle. A smile spread across Johanna's face, confidence replaced timidity. The horse turned

D Marie

his head toward her and whinnied. She laughed, looked at Ari, and said, "Let's go!"

Ari offered a faint smile, pushed down his grieving emotions, and replied. "Let's find out why the bells are ringing."

As they rode to town, Ari watched Johanna to make sure she wouldn't fall off. To his amazement, she maintained good posture as they trotted the horses down the lane. Although Johanna bobbed up and down in her saddle, she did not mind the motion at all. She beamed with delight as she partook in her new adventure.

If I ask her, will she say yes? Ari pondered with a heavy heart as they approached the town square. He watched his horse's ears twitch at the sound of the bells. His own ears ached at the noise. "Let's tie them up here," Ari said. "We can walk to the square."

As they got closer, they saw some Christanans dressed in their finer clothes. Nearby, a team of four white horses pulled a strange carriage decorated in elegant colors with gold trim. Each horse was groomed to perfection. Red plumed feathers, tucked into the braided manes, stood upright on each of the horses' heads. As the carriage slowly entered the square, two people waved from inside.

"Do you know them?" Johanna asked Ari.

"No, I have never seen them before," he replied as he marveled at the carriage.

The horses stopped in front of the royal palace. If Ari thought the carriage to be elegant, the palace was magnificent. Tall circular towers, covered with conical roofs, rose majestically from the corners. Banners of Christana waved in the wind from the peak of each roof. Guards, dressed in tunics and tabards displaying the royal crest, stood at attention on the ramparts of the palace walls. The entrance of the palace had two huge wooden doors that faced the town square. Above the doors jutted a balcony from which the royal family could easily address their subjects.

The occupants exited the carriage and stood in front of the palace. At the same time, the bells quit ringing, and the heavy curtains hanging in the king's balcony parted. The wooden and glass doors opened. King Eric approached the balcony and welcomed the people. With a loud voice, he proclaimed, "Citizens of our great kingdom of Christana, it is with great pleasure that I share with you good news. My son has returned!"

"As you know, the plague took the life of your queen, my wife. Fearing for our son's life, her last wish was to have our only child live far away and to be educated in Herrgott. Now, Prince Albert has completed his university training and has returned to us. Not only has Albert become a man ready for the duties of a king, he has found the one he wants to share his life with. My son and the lovely Princess Maria of Herrgott are engaged to be married."

The whole crowd erupted with cheers for Albert and Maria while Ari gazed at Johanna. *Her face is so lovely*, he thought.

"Isn't she beautiful?" Johanna remarked, nodding toward Maria.

"Yes, she is," replied Ari. But, he did not look at Maria. He gazed at his love, Johanna.

The palace doors slowly opened. Albert and Maria waved to the townsfolk one last time and followed the palace guards to the inside courtyard. The carriage and the accompanying Herrgott guards followed behind them. The young couple had traveled a long distance, and six days on the unpaved path took its toll. Their weary bodies succumbed to exhaustion and needed rest. The horses, pulling the carriage, hung their heads and licked their lips while they plodded toward the horse gate. Their nostrils flared as if they could smell food and water beyond the wall. When everyone had entered, the large doors closed.

Ari still hadn't taken his eyes off Johanna. "Perhaps we should go home, too, Johanna. Your mother will be wondering about all this excitement."

Reluctantly, Johanna agreed, "Yes, it's getting late."

They retrieved their horses and rode back to their homes. Ari had new hope in his heart. Although he still grieved for his father, being with Johanna gave him a comfort he never had before, and he didn't want to lose it.

Chapter 5

The Announcement

The next morning, Johanna shared the events about the royal couple with her mother. Elina's eyes lit up with amazement. As they talked, a pounding noise brought them to the window. Peering outside, they saw someone nailing a parchment onto a tree near the lane. They hastened outside to investigate.

"It's written in beautiful script," Johanna noted. "The scribes must have been writing all night."

The notice announced the wedding of the royal couple, Prince Albert and Princess Maria:

Citizens of Christana
You are cordially invited to the Wedding Reception
of
Prince Albert and Princess Maria
July 1 at 3 of the clock in the Town Square

"What shall we wear?" Johanna asked her mother. "This will be the best reception I'll ever attend."

Elina smiled. "Follow me. I have something to show you." Elina took her daughter to her room. The window curtains swayed in the gentle breeze while the morning sun filled the room with light. Next to her bed stood a wooden chest that Elina used as a table. She took the candle off the top and laid it on the floor. With nimble fingers, she released the latch and opened the chest revealing a beautiful dress.

D Marie

"I wore this when your father and I were married. Try it on, Johanna."

The dark blue cloth felt soft as Johanna lifted it out of the chest. The white lace trimming the dress instantly caught her eye—so beautiful! She held it up and noted that the top had a form-fitting bodice and waist. The full skirt flowed from the waist to the floor and had an A-shaped insert of brocade material in the front that gave the dress a royal appearance. Matching brocade fabric extended from the bottom of the blue cap sleeves to the wrists. Elina's mother had been a seamstress, too, and had made the dress for Elina many years ago. It was still as beautiful as the day Elina had worn it for her wedding.

Johanna clutched the dress with both arms then carefully put it on. "Mama, it's beautiful! Grandmother was a wonderful seamstress."

Elina smiled and fastened the hooks and eyes in the back. Turning toward the mirror with her mother by her side, Johanna saw not only the beauty of the dress, she also saw the love of a mother admiring her daughter. The dress fit perfectly.

As they savored the moment, someone knocked on the front door. Both women looked at each other in bewilderment. "Who could that be?" Elina asked. "Visitors normally don't come this early in the morning." Elina walked across the room and opened the door. "Good morning, Ari. Please come in."

When Ari walked in, he saw Johanna. He immediately stopped and stared at her. She was taken aback. *What's wrong?* she wondered. Johanna looked down and remembered what she was wearing—her mother's wedding dress.

Ari shook his head and blinked. "Forgive me, Johanna. Your kindheartedness and charm have overwhelmed my heart. I cannot keep this inside any longer." He walked toward Johanna, lowered himself to his bended knee, and placed her hand in his. "Johanna, I love you with all my heart and all my soul. I will love you forever. There will never be another who can take your place. Since the day you came with the basket of

Journey to the Glass Hill

love, I knew you were the one. My father was my life at that time, and his needs guided my days. He's gone now. Johanna, I have wanted to say these words to you many times. I tried last night but the bells started ringing.

Johanna smiled and continued to gaze into Ari's eyes.

Ari's soul groaned as he summoned the courage to ask the most important question of his life. The painful waiting would be over in a few seconds. The pounding of his heart reverberated in his ears. His hands became wet and clammy. With hope-filled eyes focused on Johanna, he asked, "Will you marry me?"

D Marie

Johanna pondered for a moment and then looked at her mother. Elina smiled and nodded. She looked at Ari again and said, "I have little to offer, because my father died so long ago. I have no dowry. What I do have, my love and my heart, I give to you forever and ever. Yes, I will marry you."

Ari wobbled as he stood up and took a deep breath. *She said yes!* The words kept echoing in his mind. He reached for her other hand, and the betrothed couple embraced for the first time.

Elina knew this day would come. Without hesitation she said, "There will be two weddings to prepare for. I wonder when the church will be available after the royal couple's wedding."

"Let's find out!" Johanna and Ari said together.

Chapter 6

The Preparations

After Johanna changed into her regular clothes, she and Ari followed the lane on their way to the church. She looked down and noticed dust clinging to the hem of her dress. *If I wear mama's dress to the royal reception, it'll get soiled for my wedding,* she thought. *I'll wear my best Sunday dress and keep the blue dress for my special day.* A big smile appeared on her face.

Ari noticed her smile and reached for her hand. He took a deep breath, looked up, and silently prayed, *Thank You, God, for giving me Johanna. How can I ever repay You?*

When they entered the church, they had to wait while the minister finished praying with one of the parishioners. "Amen," the man said and remained seated with his head down while he continued to pray.

The minister turned to the newcomers and greeted them, "Welcome, my children. It's good to see you." Reverend Gudmund focused on Ari. "Yesterday was difficult for you, and the bells ringing not long after your father's burial must have been confusing."

"It was, Reverend Gudmund," replied Ari. "We went to the square to discover what the excitement was about—a wedding for the royal couple. The prince left so many years ago that I can barely remember him. While he was away, he found the one to share his life with."

"Yes, Ari," the minister agreed, "but what troubles you?"

"I, too, have found the one to share my life with, and we want to be married."

D Marie

The minister gazed at the couple. "I have watched you two grow up. Both of you lost a parent at an early age. Ari, Johanna, you have always had love in your hearts for your family. Now you want to start a family of your own. This is a marriage the Lord loves to bless."

"Reverend," Ari began, "we do not have much. We would like a simple wedding, just our families."

Johanna nodded in agreement, and then she had to ask, her voice stuttering some, "Reverend, after the royal couple is wed, what becomes of the flowers decorating the church? If no one wants them, may we use some of the flowers for our wedding the following day?"

The minister placed his hand to the side of his face. "I'll inquire and let you know later." At that moment, the man in the pew lifted his head and nodded to the minister. Then he lowered his head and went back to his prayers.

"Thank you for helping us!" Ari and Johanna said together. In the excitement of the moment, they embraced each other.

Journey to the Glass Hill

Afterward, they shook the hand of the minister and walked hand in hand out the door. They never noticed that the man, sitting in the pew, had just given his approval to their request.

Once outside, Johanna stopped in her tracks. "Ari, I'm so sorry!"

"About what?" he asked as his heart raced again.

"I chose a day and didn't ask you!"

"Johanna, you just spoke faster than I did. If you hadn't asked, I would have. We are going to have a wonderful life together." *When it comes to you, Johanna,* Ari admitted to himself, *I give you everything I have. I never want to lose you.*

They both returned to their respective homes and started the preparations. Only four weeks remained until their wedding.

Ari wanted Johanna to be pleased with her new home, and he let her give his house the woman's touch it had needed for a long time. Elina helped by giving Johanna some of her own furnishings to adorn the rooms.

While Johanna worked inside, Ari stayed busy with work outside, mainly in the barn. It was off limits to Johanna. Ari made her promise not to peek. "What is he doing in that barn?" wondered Johanna aloud. She didn't dwell on it too much, because she had many things to do before her wedding day arrived.

Johanna surveyed the interior rooms of the house with her mother. "Mama, the rooms have been swept, but the surfaces need scrubbing. Where do I begin?"

"Start with the walls and work your way down to the floors and furniture. I'll make some new curtains with our leftover linen fabric."

The wood absorbed the clean water and released a fresh outdoor scent. Sunlight streamed through the clean window panes as a gentle breeze fluttered the new curtains.

Johanna took inventory of the food supplies, and Ari gladly went to town to pick up what the cooking room lacked. He also bought linen to make new bedding and cloths for the cooking room. There was always a need for more fabric.

It was a bittersweet time for Elina. She remembered her own preparations when she had gotten married and was happy for her daughter. The thought of being alone in her home crept into her mind, but Elina quickly chased those thoughts away. "Johanna is getting married," she told herself. "Ari is so kind and loving. He will be a devoted husband for my daughter. It's like he sets Johanna on a pedestal."

Two days before the royal wedding, Johanna gave her mother the grand tour of her new home. As she guided her mother through the house, Elina smiled. The new curtains and the furnishings that she shared with her daughter changed the once spartan looking house into an inviting home. "It's beautiful, Johanna. You did a wonderful job."

The larder contained preserved meats and fruits. Recently harvested root vegetables gave the area an earthy scent. "We have a few spices, but I may need more to help my cooking abilities," Johanna added with a wink and a smile. "Mama, I'm glad the cleaning is finished. That was tiring work."

"Your house is ready, and our clothes are ready. Let's rest tomorrow."

"Good idea. My last time to sleep in and let my Mama pamper me."

"Indeed I will," Elina assured her. As the two walked out the door, Johanna began to reminisce about her conversation with the minister.

With great pleasure, Reverend Gudmund informed Ari and Johanna that there would be some flowers left in the church for their wedding decorations, but they would not have access to the church until three of the clock. The king's servants would need the time beforehand to pack up the palace's golden candelabras, the royal banners, and other items belonging to

Journey to the Glass Hill

the palace. *It doesn't matter*, she thought. *I'm grateful to have some flowers. I wonder what color they are?*

Chapter 7

The Wedding Gift

The sun shone brightly, and wispy clouds graced the sky. Sweet scents of summer filled the air creating a perfect day for the royal wedding.

Several servants hurried back and forth from the palace decorating the town square for the invited guests. Strategically placed barricades prevented horses, carts and wagons from entering the festive area. Ari and Johanna decided to walk to town. Elina thanked them. She didn't ride horses.

The royal couple had a private, intimate wedding. Only family, friends, and the members of the Royal Court attended.

After the wedding ceremony, Albert and Maria entered their carriage, the same carriage and team of horses they had arrived in a month earlier. It was a wedding present from Maria's father. The crowd cheered the happy couple as they rode around the streets of Christana. When the carriage stopped in front of the palace entrance, the royal couple emerged, and the crowd cheered again.

Albert addressed the townsfolk, "Thank you, citizens of Christana. On one of the most important days of our lives, our wedding day, Maria and I are humbled by your thoughtfulness. In a few minutes, we will share with you the banquet prepared for this memorable day. At this time, I would like Reverend Gudmund to say a blessing for this important occasion."

Reverend Gudmund approached the royal couple and nodded in approval. "Christanans, let's bow our heads and ask for the Lord's blessing.

D Marie

"Dear Heavenly Father, this is a day like no other day we have known before. We have a young man here who places You first and not himself. Lord, may You place Your hand upon him and give him Your wisdom, not only for his life, but also for the lives that are now entrusted in his care for this is also Prince Albert's coronation day. We ask You to bless King Erik's wedding present to his son. Father, our new king is humble of heart and will not display a crown on his head to show superiority. He wants to earn the respect of Your people before that happens.

"We ask for Your blessings on our new queen. She has left the land of her birth to make Christana her new home. Queen Maria is a blessing to us."

Maria blushed as she nodded. Albert squeezed her hand.

"Lord," Gudmund continued, "we ask for Your blessing on this food we share together, and we ask for Your favor and protection on our new monarchs, King Albert and Queen Maria. In Your Name, we pray. Amen."

All eyes focused on Albert's father. The resigning king nodded his approval.

"Amen!" the people shouted simultaneously. "Long live King Albert and Queen Maria!"

The royal servants, who had been standing in front of the banquet tables, stepped behind them. After greeting the new king and queen, the hungry guests proceeded to partake of the prepared meal. Sumptuous varieties of meats laid on the tops of sliced bread. Each portion rested on a napkin that the guests could keep as a remembrance of this memorable event. Delicious, sweet tasting pastries were available on another group of tables.

Journey to the Glass Hill

Albert and Maria stood near a fountain in the town square. The bubbling water provided a cool and peaceful setting to greet the royal couple. Albert looked regal in his royal attire. Even though he was a king, he didn't have the pretense of being arrogant. He attentively listened to the people of Christana and humbly accepted their best wishes.

"We are pleased to meet you, King Albert. It has been many years since we have seen you," many of the townsfolk said.

With his sincere persona, Albert shared, "I'm looking forward to walking in our town of Christana and visiting your shops." He desired to be near his people and get to know them.

Maria kindly greeted each one of their guests. Gracefully extending her hand to each person, she gazed into their eyes as she received her wedding guests. "Congratulations, Queen Maria, and welcome to Christana," the guests shared.

"Thank you, I appreciate your kindness."

Since Maria's family was unable to attend her wedding, Maria knew no one from Christana except Albert. In one month's time, she had learned the servants' and some of the guards' names.

Initially, her royal attendants wondered how the Herrgott princess would behave. To their surprise and delight, Maria had a thoughtful and kindhearted personality. The ladies-in-waiting tried to make Maria's days as pleasant as possible. Maria noticed and often had the ladies join her in the garden or library just to share each other's company. Sometimes, they dined together for their midday meal. She treated the ladies-in-waiting with high respect.

When it was Ari's and Johanna's turn to greet the newlyweds, Johanna took off her necklace and gave the couple her locket. They opened it and saw a cross inside. As sincerely as she could, Johanna said, "May the Lord bless you and your family."

Albert and Maria marveled at the gift which they graciously accepted. Elina walked behind Ari and Johanna and recognized the locket. Salty tears stung Elina's eyes as she remembered when her husband had given her and Johanna matching lockets one Christmas long ago.

Johanna, you gave away your locket. That hurts. Please Lord bless this gift so it may benefit the receiver the same way as it has benefitted the giver. She cleared her mind when her turn came to greet the royal couple. "Your Royal Highnesses, I am Elina, your humble servant." She paused for a moment and curtsied in respect. "If there is anything I can do for you, I am at your service. God bless you both."

Albert and Maria could tell there was something special about this woman. They sensed a warm and sincere peace about her. "Thank you, Elina. We are pleased to make your acquaintance, and God bless you," Albert and Maria replied. Elina nodded. Afterward, she joined Ari and Johanna and dined on the delicious food.

Journey to the Glass Hill

As they enjoyed their meal, Johanna looked around the square. It was adorned with the banners of Christana. Flags, with embroidered crosses, were displayed everywhere to honor the wedding couple. They fluttered in a breeze revealing their vibrant colors. She gently closed her eyes, imagining what the decorated church must look like inside.

I wonder what color the flowers are? she asked herself. *They must be lovely for such a beautiful queen.*

Although they wanted to stay longer, it was getting late, and tomorrow was their big day. Ari, Johanna, and Elina returned home, reminiscing about the lovely afternoon, a royal wedding, and that they had been part of it.

Chapter 8

Big Surprise

Elina took a deep breath and announced, "It's time." Johanna nodded and quietly followed her mother. Tears gathered in their eyes. Tears of joy for the marriage and tears of sadness, for this was the last time they would share this home together. Elina quietly dabbed her daughter's eyes. Words were not necessary. Quickly, their thoughts turned to the donning of the wedding dress.

After the two women had changed their clothes, Elina fixed her daughter's hair. She laid delicate white flowers, woven into the shape of a crown, on top of Johanna's head. Her long hair laid gracefully around her shoulders with curly ringlets framing her face. The young woman stood by her mother's window and looked outside. The afternoon sunlight poured through the curtain and bathed the bride with its radiant illumination. She was ready.

Johanna and Ari wanted a small wedding. Ari had no relatives and Johanna just had her mother. The women had cooked a meal for the three of them to share after the wedding. Meat simmered in the kettle that hung in the fireplace. The bread had been baked the day before. Vegetables would not take much time and could be cooked later in the afternoon.

The two women walked into the cooking room. "Johanna, stir the kettle one more time, and I'll tend the fire." Elina peeked out the window. "I see Ari with the transportation. It's time to leave for the church."

When Johanna came out of the cottage, she caught her breath, realizing what Ari had been working on in the barn all that time. He had transformed a humble cart into a magnificent carriage. The new "carriage" had been painted white and trimmed in blue. Ari's horse was completely groomed including a braided mane. He neighed and tossed his head as if he knew Johanna would leave this cottage and come to his home. Ari sat in the cart as Johanna continued to survey it in wonder. When her eyes rested on Ari, she noticed he was dressed in his finest clothes. The curls of his hair, that usually rested on his forehead, were neatly combed into place. He looked regal and handsome.

Johanna smiled, raised her hands to her face, and exclaimed, "Ari, it's beautiful!"

"It's my wedding present for you," Ari affectionately responded. "I want the best for my angel."

The small cart was a tight fit for three people, so Ari rode his other horse which had been tethered to the back rail. He called for the horse, strapped to the cart, to walk next to him. Although Johanna held the reins, the well-trained horse would follow Ari anywhere.

"It's almost three. Do you think the king's servants will be finished removing the palace belongings?" asked Johanna. The

Journey to the Glass Hill

king had agreed to leave some of the flowers for the young couple's wedding. However, when they arrived at the church, the minister frantically ran toward them.

Ari's face turned pale. "What's wrong, Reverend Gudmund?"

"The palace servants are still packing up inside the church," said the minister with great angst in his voice. "We must wait outside."

As Ari tied off the horses, the church bell rang to announce the time—bong, bong, bong. It was three of the clock.

Slowly, the church doors opened. The servants, dressed in formal attire, motioned for the wedding couple to enter. Once inside, all four, including the minister, stood with puzzled looks. As they looked around the interior of the church, their mouths dropped open.

The royal banners that had been in the square the day before now adorned the church walls. Ribbons and bows gracefully hung over the ends of the pews. At the end of the aisle, the soft glow of candlelight covered the altar and highlighted their only request. Elegant yellow flowers surrounded the sides of the altar and candelabras. They were nestled in the white bows draped on the pews. Their delicate fragrance filled the church.

Immediately, Reverend Gudmund sized up the situation, took Ari by the hand, and led him to the front by the altar. Elina took her daughter by the hand and led her to the back of the aisle. Promptly, as if on cue, violin music filled the church. *I will treasure this day forever,* Johanna thought.

Reverend Gudmund nodded for the women to come forward. Elina squeezed her daughter's hand and accompanied Johanna up the aisle. They walked slowly. Elina was not in a hurry to let her only child go.

Johanna cherished the moment and reflected, *I want to fill my senses with all these sights, sounds, and fragrances. This is more than I could ever imagine.*

"Mama, I feel like a princess."

"Johanna, you are a princess. Our new king is kind and thoughtful. Someday, I hope we can do something to repay him. Right now, your prince is waiting for you."

Elina placed her daughter's hand into Ari's hand. It was the Lord's turn to seal the bond between this man and woman.

When the minister completed the ceremony, Ari and Johanna kissed for the first time as husband and wife. Suddenly, Ari's stomach growled. "That was embarrassing," Ari admitted. "I forgot to eat today. I've been busy getting my house—" Ari paused and looked at Johanna, "—*our* home freshened up."

As they walked out of the church, the royal servants held the door open for them. Ari and Johanna stopped and thanked them. The servants assured the couple their words of gratitude would be relayed to the royal family.

Elina turned to her daughter and said, "It's time for you to go for a ride for the first time as husband and wife."

Ari's feet barely touched the ground as he left to retrieve the cart. Johanna turned to her mother and asked, "Mama, what about you and Ari's horse?"

"Don't be concerned about me. The Lord will provide."

Ari returned with the "wedding carriage." He disembarked from the cart to get Johanna. After helping her up, Ari returned to the driver's side, picked up the reins, and started to leave.

"The evening meal will be at six. See you then," Elina called after them.

"We won't be late!" Johanna and Ari replied together, and off they went.

Elina watched and waved until the road turned and the corner building blocked her view. She looked at the remaining horse and sighed. The minister came outside and joined her. "Reverend, we're having an evening meal at six tonight. You're welcome to join us."

"Thank you. With two weddings in a row, I haven't had much time to cook."

Journey to the Glass Hill

"Good," replied Elina. "We'll see you then."

As Elina walked toward the horse, the minister asked, "Do you ride a horse now?"

"Oh, no! I'm going to walk him home."

"Please, take my horse and cart. I'll ride your horse later."

Elina gave him a grateful smile. "Thank you, Reverend Gudmund."

She mounted the cart, took the reins, and guided the horse and cart to her home. "The Lord provides," Elina whispered.

Ari and Johanna heard the church bell ring six times as they came down the lane to Elina's house. When Johanna saw Ari's horse, she knew her mother was there. When she saw the other horse and cart, her eyes opened wide. *Who else is here?* she wondered.

Elina and the minister walked out the door. "Right on time!" noted Elina. "The food is ready."

As Johanna walked by her mother, Elina whispered, "The Lord provides."

Johanna smiled and prayed. *Lord, thank You. I know You will tend to my mother's needs now that she will be living alone.*

The setting sun slipped behind the tree line and the moon appeared. Leaving the only home she had known and start a new one tore at Johanna's heart. Ari sensed it and said, "You can come here as often as you like. My only request is always come back to me."

At this tender sharing of love, Reverend Gudmund gave the newlyweds the Lord's blessing, "May the Lord bless you and keep you. May the Lord make His face shine upon you and be gracious to you. May the Lord lift up His countenance upon you and give you peace. Live long my children, and let the Lord be with you always. Amen."

Johanna kissed and hugged her mother goodbye. Ari kissed his new mother-by-marriage goodbye. Both hugged the minister.

D Marie

As the happy couple headed down the lane to start their new life together, Elina sighed. *Oh, how I wish my husband was here right now*, she thought and took another deep breath. Sensing the emotional moment, the minister put his arm around Elina's shoulders and whispered, "Elina, the Lord is with you, and I'm here for you, too.

Chapter 9

New Direction

Smoke rose from the chimney. Ari's mouth watered thinking about his evening meal as he watched Johanna walk down the lane to her mother's cottage. The corners of his mouth turned up as he envisioned the two women chatting together. Later in the day, Johanna took Ari a cool drink of water. His face lit up. She always came back to him.

"How did I get so lucky to have you?" he asked.

Johanna blushed. "The Lord provides."

During the evening meal, Johanna noticed a worried look on Ari's face. "What's wrong, Ari? Can I help?"

"I want to give you more than what we have, but we only make a small profit from the crops and animals we sell. What if we have a bad year, and we don't take in enough coins?"

"Ari, I do not need much, but it is a concern. Let's pray about it. The Lord will provide an answer." Ari and Johanna held hands.

"Johanna, will you pray? I don't pray very well, and this is a serious request," pleaded Ari.

"Of course," Johanna said with confidence. "Dear Father, You are a gracious and kind Father. You know our needs even before we ask. We thank You for helping and guiding us in what You would have us do to increase our income. This we ask in Jesus' Name…" But, before she could say the word, Amen, the dog barked several times.

"Amen," Ari quickly blurted. "I'll go see what he's barking about." Ari opened the door. "The horse is loose, and he's walking around. I'll be right back as soon as I get him in the barn."

"That's it," cried out Johanna as she followed Ari out the door. "Thank You, Lord."

"You're thanking God because our horse is loose?" questioned Ari.

"No, I'm thanking Him for showing us the new direction for our lives!"

"New direction?" teased Ari. "As in going to the barn?"

"Silly man. Ari, what do you love very much?"

"You!"

"Besides me?"

"Your mother?" Ari replied hoping he had guessed correctly this time.

"Ari, horses! You are so talented in training horses. You taught me how to overcome my inability to ride. You designed

Journey to the Glass Hill

a beautiful cart for us to use. Ari, people will want to employ your talents. We could even start raising horses to train and sell."

Ari's eyes widened as he raised his eyebrows. Then he relaxed and smiled. "Johanna, this is a great idea. What would I do without you?"

"Go on a journey," she replied.

"A journey?" Ari turned a puzzled face to her. "A journey to where?"

"To find me of course!" Johanna smiled as she walked back into the house.

"That's my girl," Ari said. He led his horse to the barn as he hummed a happy tune and wondered, *Where do I start with this new direction?*

Later that night, Johanna had something else to share. "Ari?"

"Yes, Dear?"

"Will our cart fit three people?"

Turning his head toward her direction, Ari gave his undivided attention. "Johanna, are you saying what I think you're saying?"

"Yes!" she said with great emphasis watching for his reaction.

He studied her face and smiled. "When?"

"In the spring."

"A baby!" Ari exclaimed. "Thank You, God. A new baby and a new direction."

The next day, Ari and Johanna went to Elina's cottage for a visit. She was pleased to see them as life was lonely at times. Elina put away the fabric pieces she had been sewing together. All three of them sat at the table.

"Mama," Johanna began, "how are you today?"

"Wonderful now that you two are here." Elina noticed that both had an odd playful look on their faces.

D Marie

Johanna couldn't hold it in any longer and asked, "Did you save any of my baby clothes?"

Elina knew exactly what that meant. "Thank You, Lord, that I am blessed to see my daughter's child. Yes, yes, I saved them all." She walked over and hugged her daughter. "Congratulations."

"Elina," Ari added, "you will be the only Mawmaw for the baby."

"Mawmaw," she repeated with a smile. "I like that name."

Chapter 10

New Addition

Humming a cheerful tune, Elina walked to her daughter's home. Help was on the way. Ari gave a big sigh of relief when she arrived. Making a cradle for the new baby and starting his new business of horse training consumed his time. It amazed him that so many women wanted to learn how to ride a horse, including Elina.

One Sunday at church, King Albert and Queen Maria congratulated Ari and Johanna on their coming child. The royal couple noted a slight tense look in Elina's eyes. As the king and queen walked out of the church, Elina summoned her courage and approached them.

"Your Majesty, you are a fair and good sovereign. If I have favor in your presence, may I make a request?" Elina asked.

"Please continue," King Albert replied.

"Johanna's child is due in a few months. I suspect that her health may be compromised. Could you have the Court Physician look at her?" Elina implored.

"He will be there tomorrow, Elina," King Albert assured her.

"Thank you, your Highness. She is my only child. For your kindness, I will pray for you and your child every day of my life."

This blessing encouraged him as he and Maria longed for a child. "Thank you for your prayers, Elina. We will pray for Johanna and her baby, too."

Elina bowed to the monarchs and went outside. "Ari, Johanna, I have good news." Elina shared as she climbed into the cart. "The Court Physician will honor us with a visit tomorrow."

"Mama, how are we going to pay him?"

"It's already been taken care of," Elina assured her.

The following day, the Court Physician arrived at Ari's and Johanna's home. Elina was there, too. He examined Johanna privately. Then he allowed Ari and Elina to enter the room.

"It's rare," he said, "but I have seen a few cases of this."

Ari's mouth went dry, and his face turned pale. Thoughts of Johanna being ill like his father had been in his last days overwhelmed Ari's mind.

The physician noticed the cradle near Johanna's bed and pointed to it. "Did you make this, Ari?"

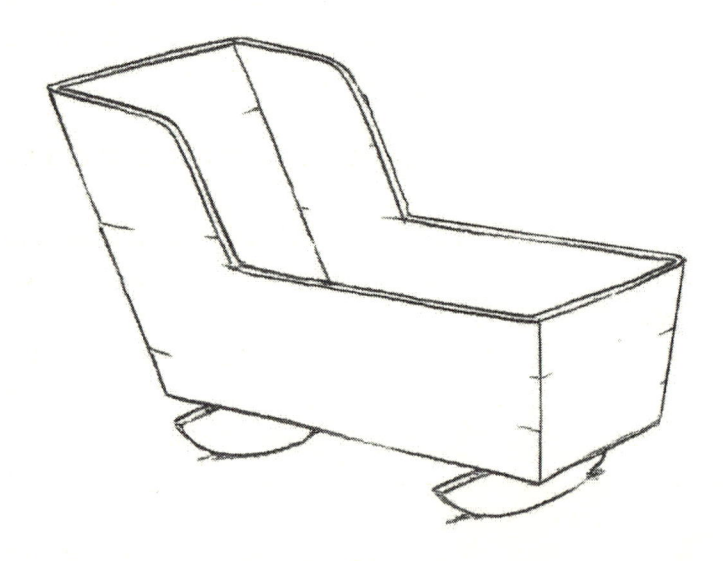

"Yes, Sire."

The physician smiled. "You better get busy then. You're going to need another."

"What? Two babies? Johanna is going to be all right?"

"Yes, but she needs complete bed rest," the physician declared. "Johanna, you may get up three or four times a day,

Journey to the Glass Hill

but only for a few minutes. The babies will take most of your energy. I will come once a week to check on your progress."

Ari thanked the physician and walked him to the door. Elina held her daughter's hand and promised, "I will be here every day for you."

"Thank you, Mama. How did you know that I needed a physician?"

"Caring for your child doesn't stop when she gets married and leaves your home. I can see your movements are slowing down, so I did it for the both of us."

The next day, when Johanna got up for her short walk, she noticed Ari going to town with the cart. After a few minutes, she was ready to lie down again. In the afternoon, she saw Ari coming back with a wagon. Johanna assessed the difference. *It's much bigger than the cart. We can all ride in it, but it's not as lovely as our wedding carriage. I'll miss it.*

One afternoon, Elina looked out the door and saw Ari by the porch and yelled, "It's time!"

Ari had just completed the final touches on the second cradle. He dropped his tools, saddled his horse, and rode as fast as he could to town to get the Court Physician.

When the two arrived, the physician asked Ari to wait outside Johanna's room. While Ari waited, he brought in the second cradle he had been working on earlier in the day. The curved boards on the bottom were now smooth, and it rocked back and forth with ease.

Sitting down, Ari tapped his foot on the floor. He stopped when he heard a baby crying. After a few moments, the physician walked out with the new baby and announced, "Ari, you have a son!"

Ari held him as the physician went back into the room. "You're so big, I will call you Magnus," Ari told his son. Ari noticed the baby had brown hair similar to his own. The baby's head was all he could see as his arms and body were tightly wrapped in a swaddling blanket.

After a few more minutes, Elina came out with another baby and said, "Ari, you have another son."

Ari tenderly put Magnus in the new cradle and took the second baby from Elina. He saw the resemblance to Magnus. "Twins! I have twin sons." The blanket was loose, and the startled baby waved his arms and legs in a jerky movement. "You look strong like a warrior, I will call you Ivar," the new father declared with great pride, pronouncing the name as EE-var. "Two sons and a wonderful wife. How could I want for anything else?" He looked up. "How is Johanna?"

"She's fine, but tired," Elina replied. "You can come in now."

Elina picked up Magnus while Ari rewrapped Ivar. They stood side by side with the babies securely nestled in their arms. Soft downy brown hair covered the babies' heads. Their oval shaped faces bore the chin cleft of their father. They momentarily opened their eyes to reveal their color, brown. They were indeed identical twins.

The proud father laid Ivar in Johanna's arm. Elina laid Magnus in the other arm. Johanna wanted to see her babies more completely. She and Ari loosened the boys' blankets, admired their new sons, and counted their fingers and toes. Both babies were fast asleep.

"You need to get some rest, too," the physician noted with a smile. "They will be waking up soon and often." Everyone quietly chuckled. It had been a long day.

Elina accompanied the physician to the door and pulled out a letter she had written the prior week. She gave the correspondence to him and said, "Please give this to the king and queen. They have been so gracious to us." He took it and departed.

King Albert and Queen Maria acknowledged the kind and thoughtful heart of Elina as they read her letter:

Journey to the Glass Hill

Your Royal Majesties,
King Albert and Queen Maria,

Thank you for allowing the Court Physician to attend to my daughter, Johanna. I will pray every day for you to have a son and daughter, too.

Your Humble Servant,
Elina

Chapter 11

Another Addition

The wagon creaked as it rolled. Perspiration gathered on Ari's hands, and he wiped them on his pants. Thoughts about his newest passengers, his newborn sons, flooded his mind. As he held the reins, Johanna and Elina held the twins. *So far, so good,* he assured himself.

One of the wheels slipped into a rut on the rugged lane jostling the whole wagon and everyone in it. The startled babies flailed their arms and wailed. Ari threw an apologetic look at his family and whispered, "Sorry."

Elina and Johanna bounced the babies up and down then rocked their bodies back and forth trying to soothe the boys. The babies calmed down and slept the rest of the way to church.

At the end of the service, Reverend Gudmund stood by the baptismal font waiting to begin the holy sacrament. Elina, the boys' grandmother, stood witness. When the minister asked for a male witness, Ari's best customer, Oskar, volunteered. "Maybe the boys will help me with my horses someday," he said with a sheepish grin. The congregation laughed, but Johanna and Ari beamed while their sons rested quietly in their arms.

Elina noticed a tear on the queen's face. Albert put his hand on his wife's hand and gently squeezed it as she wiped her tear away. He softly whispered to her, "The Lord will provide a child for us." They set aside their desires and smiled as they were truly happy for the new parents.

Elina turned her attention toward the twins. Hunger and tiredness overtook the babies' pleasant disposition, and they cried. After the family returned home, Elina prepared the meal while Johanna rocked and fed the babies.

"Mama, I'm so appreciative of your help. You are a blessing. Magnus and Ivar are healthy boys, and they take most of my energy to care for them."

"I'm grateful to be here. I get to see my grandsons and you all the time."

Ari wavered between being grateful for Elina's help and being jealous of her. Although he wanted to be in the house with his wife and sons, his business had grown and demanded more of his time. In addition to the fields and farm animals, he had to take care of a new team of horses.

Time went by quickly. The boys turned four and kept each other occupied as Johanna tended to the needs of the house. One day as Johanna prepared the food, she asked the boys to go get their father.

"Papa, Papa! Mama needs you!" they yelled, running to the chicken coop.

Ari looked up and dropped the feed bucket. Chickens flocked to his feet blocking his path. With one quick jump over the fence, he ran to the house. Ari's heart pounded in his chest when he found Johanna collapsed on the floor. As he picked her up, he cried out to the boys, "Go get your grandmother." Holding Johanna tightly, he carried her into the bedroom.

The boys made the short trip as fast as they could. Gasping for air, the twins trembled as they stood in the doorway. Their eyes pleaded for help. Elina immediately dropped her sewing and rushed to the door. She ran down the lane with the boys who tried to keep up with her. *What is wrong?* she wondered. Entering the house, Elina paused, breathed deeply, and walked to the bedroom.

Journey to the Glass Hill

Johanna sat up in bed while Ari stood by her side. Both smiled. "Johanna, Ari?" Elina asked with a puzzled look.

"Mama," Johanna exclaimed, "I'm all right. The baby is making me tired."

Elina's eyes opened wide. After a deep breath, her shoulders dropped and her tension subsided. With wobbly legs, she walked to her daughter's side. God bless you and the new baby."

"Baby!" the twins yelled. Magnus and Ivar looked at each other and grinned. "We want a brother."

After Reverend Gudmund concluded the service with a prayer, Elina gathered her thoughts and approached the king for help. "Your Majesty," pleaded Elina, "if I may, I ask for your favor once again for my daughter. She is with child and has need of your physician. In return, I will watch over your child when that day comes."

King Albert remembered the vow Elina had made to pray for him and Queen Maria to have a child four years ago. Now, Elina would bless them with her tender care, too. "Elina," the king responded, "your loving and kind spirit is well known in Christana, and there is no other person the queen and I would want to care for our child more than you. We know the Lord will provide. Please take the Court Physician and tend to your daughter."

"Thank you for your kindness, King Albert," she replied.

The Court Physician prescribed the same treatment; Johanna needed bed rest. Elina arrived every day to help and never complained.

"Elina, I'm so thankful," Ari shared. "Without you, we would suffer."

"That's what family does," she replied.

To keep the twins busy, Elina began to teach them how to read. The boys wanted to learn, but had difficulty staying on task. Being creative, she made up games and songs to keep their attention. Soon, Magnus and Ivar could read simple words and sentences.

When the special day arrived, Elina went outside and announced, "Ari, it's time!"

Ari had a horse saddled and ready at all times. He quickly rode to the palace, and the Court Physician followed him back to his home.

Ari and the twins waited in the front room while the physician and Elina attended to Johanna. Magnus' and Ivar's

Journey to the Glass Hill

eyes were full of wonder as their father explained what the baby would look like.

"The baby will be very small, like the other farm animals when they are born."

"Will the baby walk the first day just like a baby horse?" Magnus asked.

"It may take a year for the baby to walk," Ari explained. "Each baby is different. You two are twins, but you are both different in your abilities."

"Can we play with the baby?" asked Ivar.

"At first, you can hold the baby and talk to the little one," Ari replied. "When the child is older, you can play some games."

Ari had more to share, but he stopped talking. High-pitched crying came from the bedroom. Three pairs of eyes watched the door.

Elina opened the door and invited Ari and the twins to come in. Although Ari had both cradles in the room, he only needed one. A new son joined their family. When Johanna held her son, Ari noticed how much he looked like her. The baby had golden hair and blue eyes exactly like his mother. "Can we name him Johann?" he asked, pronouncing the name as YO-hahn.

"Yes," she agreed. "Thank you, Ari. Johann will be my gift to you."

Johanna looked at her older sons and invited them to come and see their new brother. Magnus placed his finger near Johann's tiny hand. The baby waved his arm around and momentarily clasped Magnus' finger. Magnus' chest puffed up with pride.

Ivar squeezed between his two brothers to get closer to the baby. Fascination filled his eyes. This baby appeared little and helpless but looked kind at the same time. Ivar patted the tiny arm. Johann turned his head and looked at him. After a while, the baby closed his eyes and fell asleep.

D Marie

Two weeks passed before Johanna could move around the house. She wanted to get up but didn't have the strength or energy. Concerned about her daughter's health, Elina had moved into the boys' room to help with the baby during the night.

"I love you, Mama," Johanna said one afternoon as she watched her mother tirelessly working in the cooking room.

Elina's knees wobbled, and she took refuge by sitting next to her daughter. She tucked that point of time away in her heart and gazed at her only child. "I love you, my daughter." They remained quiet for several minutes treasuring the moment.

When Johann was a month old, Johanna felt strong enough to attend church for his baptism. Elina stood by the baptismal font as a witness. When the minister called for a male witness, to Johanna's and Ari's amazement, the king stood up. Albert looked at his wife.

Maybe the Lord will bless us somehow through this child, Maria thought, and she nodded her approval.

King Albert announced, "I will." Johann's godfather would be the king. Magnus and Ivar watched from the pew as their brother received the baptismal waters and the promises of God.

"Our brother didn't cry," Magnus noted.

"He is a good brother," Ivar added.

The family returned home. Johanna rested as her mother cooked the midday meal. Ari played with the twins. He never commented, but he had an uneasy feeling about Johanna's health. "God, help my Johanna. Please. I'll be forever grateful. It hurts to see her this way."

Chapter 12

Tragedy Strikes

By sheer physical strength and size, he was the strongest person in the room, but he lost the fight and gave up. His eyelids won, and they drooped again. Thoughts of taking a nap drifted through Ari's mind as he rubbed his face.

"Papa, wake up," Magnus shouted.

"Did the baby keep you awake last night?" Ivar asked. "Should Grandma stay with us again?"

Forcing his eyes open, the tired father noticed Johanna trying to disguise her yawn as she held the little baby. "Come on, boys," Ari called. "Let's go outside." Looking affectionately at Ari, Johanna smiled as the boys followed their father out the door. Ari kept the twins with him during the day to give Johanna more time to focus on their newest arrival.

At the age of five, the twins had manageable chores. Ari noticed how easily they interacted with the animals. Magnus and Ivar mimicked their father with the work. A few wisps of hay managed to stay on their pitchforks as they carried the dried grass to the stalls. A big smile appeared on Ari's face. "Well done, boys," the proud father said, and he hugged his sons.

Ari led the boys to the chicken coop. The twins smiled until their father held out the bucket of feed in their direction. Magnus and Ivar took a step backward. They didn't want to get chicken droppings on their shoes.

"When you get older," Ari began. "I'll get you both a pair of boots. For today, keep your rawhide straps tied tight, or your shoes will come off."

D Marie

"Icky," Magnus squealed.

"Can't we pour the feed on the ground by the fence?" Ivar asked.

"Would you want to eat your food on a dirty floor?" his father responded.

"No," Ivar replied hoping his father would take pity on him.

"Then, give it a try. We have plenty of soap and water," Ari assured him with a wink.

"What about Magnus?"

"He goes in tomorrow."

Magnus' tranquil eyes immediately opened wide. He had hoped his father had forgotten about him. "Thanks a lot, Ivar."

Ivar tightened his straps, grabbed the feed bucket, and ventured into the chicken yard. When he returned, his shoes were still on his feet. He gave his brother a smug grin as he wiped his shoes on the grass and said, "Your turn is tomorrow."

Ari smiled. He sought a quiet area by a tree and laughed. Then, he prayed, "Thank you, God, for my children. My life is going to get easier with their help. Please put Your hand on Johanna and make her stronger. She has not been her normal self since Johann was born."

An idea came to Ari as he watched the horses grazing in the pasture. *I'll carve a wooden horse for Johann. He'll be working with me one day, too.*

Ivar fidgeted in his seat. Magnus tapped his fingers on the table. With a cocked eyebrow, their mother threw them "the look," and they both settled down. "Each of you must read one more paragraph," Johanna requested.

The left corners of their mouths pulled down in a slight pucker. Their mother cocked another eyebrow in return. The race was on to finish their morning reading lesson.

Johanna listened as her sons finished. "Well done. You may go."

Journey to the Glass Hill

The boys made it out the doorway before their mother could pick up the book. A new race began. Who would find their father first? Both waved at their grandmother as she approached the house.

Elina entered the cooking room ready to help. "Good morning, Johanna. How are you today?"

"Good morning, Mama," Johanna responded in her cheeriest voice. "I'm wonderful." She didn't want her mother to worry and hid the truth.

With two women doing the work, Johanna disguised her lack of energy from everyone—especially Ari. Most of the day, he worked outside. In the evening, he played with his boys.

Standing at her cottage door, Elina took a deep breath as she read the courier's letter. One of her prayers for King Albert and Queen Maria had been answered. The royal couple expected a child to join their family in a few months. Happiness filled her heart, but a queasy feeling began to grow in her gut. Going to the palace to help care for the queen meant leaving Johanna to do all the housework, and Johann was still a little boy.

The swift-footed, two-year-old watched the doorway waiting for his attack. The next person who entered the house became a target for a hug. When his brother walked in, Johann's momentum knocked him off his feet. Ivar brushed away the long, blond hair hiding Johann's face and hugged him back. As Johann's hair grew longer, he looked even more like his mother.

After Ivar left the house, Johann played with the toy horse his father made for him. He pretended to be a trainer like his papa. Learning to speak in sentences at an early age, Johann repeated everything he heard just like a parrot. "You're a fine-looking horse. Are you ready for your workout? Let's go."

Johanna sighed as she watched her youngest son. *I wish I had time to play with him*, she thought. *I'm behind already. I have to keep working.*

D Marie

One Sunday afternoon, during the twins' reading lessons, Johanna collapsed to the floor. Scared, the twins ran outside to get their father.

"Papa, Papa!" they cried. "Mama fell!"

Ari instinctively knew that this time her collapse was serious, and he ran with all his might and yelled over his shoulder, "Grandma is home! Go tell her to get the physician immediately! Take a horse with you!"

The twins ran down the lane to their grandmother's house pulling a horse behind them. When they were close to the door, they cried out, "Mama is hurt!" Elina immediately came out of the cottage and saw their tear-stained faces.

"Get the physician! Please hurry!" the boys pleaded.

Elina knew she had to reach the palace quickly. She looked at the horse, noting that the children had forgotten to saddle it—not that they could have done so anyway. *Well, no time to worry about that now*, she thought.

Magnus steadied the horse while Ivar fetched a stool. Their grandmother gathered her skirt and mounted the horse. With the reins in hand, Elina rode to town.

To see Elina ride a horse was unusual. To see her ride bareback was alarming. As she approached the town square, the palace guards assisted her and summoned the Court Physician. He took another horse, and they both rode together back to Ari's farm.

As they entered the house, they found Ari sitting on the floor holding Johanna in his arms, and he cried out, "No, Johanna, no. Don't go!"

Johanna had passed on. The twins leaned on their father and cried with him.

Johann stood and pleaded, "Mama, wake up!"

Magnus and Ivar understood, but little Johann did not. He sat on the floor and laid his head on her lap.

Journey to the Glass Hill

Elina slumped to the floor. Her beloved child was gone. *Why wasn't I here for her?* she wondered brokenly.

The physician got on his knees to console the family. He put his arms around Ari and the boys, but his efforts produced no comfort. With deep sorrow, he gave his condolences. "Ari, Elina, boys, I'm so sorry for your loss." As he walked out the door, he pondered on the situation. *There was no fever, no rashes, no illness, just lack of energy. Could it have been a weak heart?* He lowered his head, mounted his horse, and returned to town.

Ari quietly listened to Reverend Gudmund as he presided over the burial. His anger mounted with each virtue describing Johanna. His heart ached, and his head hurt. He could not hold back his emotions any longer.

After the burial, Ari thrust his fist to the sky and raised his voice. "You took the love of my life away. Now, I take my love from You. I prayed to You asking for Your help. You didn't help us. From this day forward, I will never go to Your church again!" Ari's soul was so crushed that bitterness and resentment found plenty of room to grow in his hurting heart.

Ari could not understand why his beloved wife had to die. He recalled how Johanna had taken a longer time to recuperate after Johann was born. *Is that what caused her to die?* he surmised. *Johanna was all right until Johann came along.* Now, Ari looked at the little boy with resentment. His heart blamed him.

How am I going to care for this two-year-old boy? Ari said to himself. *Elina is working in the palace and will not be able to help. On the other hand, the twins are older and can take care of themselves.*

Elina sensed his depression and offered her assistance. "Ari, if you need help, I can take the young boy with me and care for him."

D Marie

This sounds like a good idea. Ari thought. *I want the twins to stay as they are helpful with the farm work.*

"Thank you, Elina. It will be difficult for me to take care of him and do my work."

"I will come for him later in the day. I need to go to town first."

"I'll have his things ready when you return."

Elina went to see the king and queen. With sad eyes and heavy heart, Maria instinctively took Elina's hands, walked closer, and hugged her friend. Elina wept uncontrollably. After Elina shared about Johann staying with her, Maria stepped backward and spoke, "We release you from your promise."

"Thank you, my queen. If it is permissible, may I bring Johann to the palace with me?"

Albert looked at Maria. She nodded. Their eyes sparkled. "Yes," Albert said. "We insist Johann be with our child as much as possible when that day arrives."

"If Ari agrees, I'll bring Johann tomorrow," Elina replied.

Elina consulted Ari, and he agreed. "I'm grateful for your help, Elina."

Quietly to himself he reasoned, *I hope this will help. I want to lose myself in my work.*

Elina gathered Johann's belongings and took him to her home. The confused little boy looked at the familiar surroundings of his grandmother's house, but his troubled heart couldn't make sense of the quick changes in his life.

Getting on her knees, Elina looked into her grandson's blue eyes. "I have a surprise for you tomorrow."

"What is it?" Johann asked.

"If I tell you, it will no longer be a surprise," his grandmother replied forcing a smile. She pulled him closer and held him in her arms.

They both picked at their evening meal as they watched the sunlight fade away. When Johann yawned, his grandmother reached for his hand and took him upstairs. Elina tucked the

Journey to the Glass Hill

young boy into his new bed. The same bed his mother used to sleep in. Tears welled in her eyes as she watched her grandchild fall asleep. Putting her grief aside, she focused on Johann's feelings, and prayed for help. "Lord, I know You can make something good out of every situation for those who love You. I love You, Lord, and I put my trust in Your Word and promise. Help us. In Jesus' Name, I pray. Amen."

When Johann woke up the next morning, he immediately asked, "What's my surprise?"

"It's waiting for us in town. Let's get ready and go."

The grieving grandmother walked outside and bit her lip trying to hold back her tears. "I want to grieve, but I can't right now. Help me Jesus," she pleaded, and the Lord provided. Peace blanketed Elina. Tranquility spread throughout her body. She went back inside and took Johann by the hand. The two of them started their journey to town.

Johann had seen the palace before, but he had never been near the doors. His eyes widened when he realized he was going inside the palace. He tightly held his grandmother's hand and walked close by her side. A guard greeted Elina and Johann at the entrance doors and escorted them into the palace courtyard. The vastness of the open space mesmerized Johann. Picturesque trees, flowers, statues, and fountains captivated his attention. Neatly trimmed grass was everywhere. He didn't have time to keep looking as the guard took them through the main doors.

Elina knew where the queen rested and guided Johann down the main hallway. Large tapestries hung from the ceiling to the floor. Matching chairs were meticulously positioned near the doors in the never-ending hallway. Tables adorned with statues and vases were placed next to the chairs. All the sights overwhelmed the little boy.

Johann's eyes wondered all over the hall when he saw a moving figure coming around the corner. Displaying a joyful smile, King Albert called to the young child in a gentle tone,

D Marie

"Johann, welcome my boy!" King Albert had a box for Johann. He carefully laid the box on the floor and sat in one of the chairs. Cautiously, Johann opened the present and broke out with a huge smile.

"A puppy!" he exclaimed. "What is his name?"

"He doesn't have one yet," answered King Albert. "What do you want to name *your* puppy?"

"My puppy?" Johann gasped. "Grandma, may I keep him?"

"Yes, my dear one," Elina reassured him. Elina's tears welled in her eyes as she looked at King Albert. She laid her hand over her heart and said, "Thank you."

He smiled and bowed his head in respect to her.

Chapter 13

Royal Arrival

Johann quickly ate his morning meal. The anticipation of the next activity toyed at his mind. The little boy waited outside watching the lane. Dust began to rise in the distance. The carriage would soon be there. King Albert provided transportation for Elina and Johann. He also provided for Johann's father and his brothers and sent them cooked meals when Elina and Johann returned home.

Ari appreciated the food. Cooking required precious time he couldn't spare, and he wasn't a good cook. When he saw Elina and Johann walking down the lane, he sent Magnus and Ivar to take their empty containers to Elina before she got close to the house. The twins exchanged the containers and scampered to the house with the food. Ari waved at Elina and Johann from a distance and returned to the barn.

As soon as Ari entered the barn, he leaned his shoulder on the doorframe. *Seeing the child reminds me of my Johanna.* Ari pressed his hand hard over his heart. *I can't get close to him, later, but not now.*

Johann looked at his grandmother with mournful eyes, another day of rejection. Elina offered a quick, quiet prayer and gritted her teeth. She walked toward the barn. Ari caught a glance of the two, quickly mounted his saddled horse, and rode past them.

"Elina, I have business in town. Please share the food with the boys while I'm gone."

"Of course, Ari." His actions caught her off guard. At least she could spend time with the twins and see all three of her grandsons together.

After the meal, the sun hid behind the tree line. Soon, the sky darkened, and the moon offered a dimmer illumination. "Boys, it's time for bed. Change your clothes."

"Grandma," Johann began, "I don't have any bedclothes here."

"You can wear one of my shirts," Magnus offered.

"Thank you," Johann mildly replied. He would have to go to bed without seeing his father, again.

After all the boys fell asleep, Ari returned. When he walked into his house, he lowered his head. Perhaps, he felt shame for his behavior. "Thank you for being with the boys, Elina. Johann will be confused if he wakes up here. I'll carry him as I walk you home."

Johann never woke up as his father carried him. Elina never said a word except to bid Ari goodnight when he left her house. She watched him in the moonlight as he walked down the lane. When the lane turned, the faint nighttime light and the barn conspired together to block her view. Ari disappeared into the night.

Elina occasionally carried the food all the way to Ari's house, ignoring the pleas of Magnus and Ivar to take the food from her. Ari seemed to anticipate her attempts. His response was always the same. He had business in town to attend to, and she could stay with the boys until he returned.

Although Elina never spoke about Ari's behavior, the king knew about the strained relationship between Johann and Ari. He missed seeing Ari and the twins at church. Albert thanked the Lord that Johann could come and worship with his grandmother.

While Elina took care of Queen Maria, Johann stayed close to his grandmother. The queen and Elina sometimes

Journey to the Glass Hill

embroidered to pass the time. Both women had excellent stitching skills. Elina enjoyed this activity since she no longer had time to make clothing for her wages. She now earned her wages at the palace.

One of Elina's sewing projects was an alphabet sampler. As she embroidered, Johann's curiosity caused him to ask about the designs. Elina named the letter and its corresponding sound. Johann repeated it.

"He is just like a parrot," Maria declared.

"Grandma, that's what Mama said!" remarked Johann.

"I'm so sorry," said Maria. "I misspoke."

"No need to apologize. We talk about Johanna every day. It helps us to keep her alive in our hearts," Elina shared. "It is like the disciples sharing the Good News of Jesus after He died and rose again. It keeps His time with us alive and our hope alive to be with Him and Johanna again."

"Thank you, Elina. You are the dearest woman I know," remarked Queen Maria. "Albert and I are blessed to have you to take care of me and our child."

Then Maria turned toward Johann and asked, "You are three now, would you like to learn how to read?"

"Yes!" he replied.

"Splendid! You and I will begin tomorrow," the queen told him.

"Thank you, your Highness," replied Elina. "I am overwhelmed how you and King Albert have shown kindness for my family."

"It's meant to be. The Lord provides," Maria added.

Johann sat patiently in his chair, and eagerly absorbed his reading lessons. King Albert noticed, too. "He is a bright child and learns quickly. Perhaps he will want to work in the palace someday," Albert said softly to himself.

The anticipated day arrived. King Albert paced the floor several times, then he sat down. He wiped his clammy hands on his pants.

Elina, who sat next to King Albert in the hallway, put her hand on his and gently patted it and said, "The Lord provided."

Her words went straight to his heart. King Albert got on his knees and prayed, "My Lord, You have blessed me many times, and I am so thankful. You have listened to our humble prayers and blessed Maria and me with a child. I pray Your servant will be a good and loving father as You are a good and loving Father. Amen."

They heard a high-pitched noise, a crying baby. The child was born, but the crying abruptly stopped. King Albert turned pale. He stood up and stared at the nearby door.

Johann walked over to the king. "She doesn't need to cry. She's a good daughter."

Elina and King Albert both looked at each other. Elina finally spoke, "Johann!"

But, before she uttered another word, the three-year-old reassured them, "I know Grandma. I know."

At that moment, the Court Physician opened the door, smiled, and congratulated the king. Albert nodded and quickly walked to his wife. He looked at Maria as she smiled. Then, he looked down at her arms. A tiny, perfectly formed face quietly looked at him. The baby was snuggly wrapped in a white blanket that contained the royal crest embroidered on the front.

Maria had placed a subtle hint of their child's gender on the pillow. *Albert should be able to figure this one without my help,* she thought.

"A tiara!" he exclaimed. "A girl! I have a daughter!" Albert's loud voice traveled to the hallway and everyone heard him.

Journey to the Glass Hill

"The Lord provided," Elina said as she waited in the hall.
"A girl!" Johann quickly added, and he went to find his puppy, Rex.

Chapter 14

A New Home

Albert gazed at his little baby girl. His eyes surveyed every feature of her face. Light colored hair complimented her blue eyes. "Maria, she's beautiful. What shall we name our daughter?"

"Your mother was named Dorothea, she pronounced the name as Do-ro-TAY-uh. We could name our little princess after her," Maria offered.

"My little princess," marveled Albert to himself as he pondered on the name. "Dorothea is an honorable name. It means a gift from God. She is a gift from God, but the name is so long."

In a louder voice, Albert said, "Dorothea is a good and proper given name for her christening, but could we call her Tea?" He pronounced the name as TAY-uh.

"Tea is an affectionate name. Yes, our daughter is Princess Tea."

Elina entered the room and presented the royal parents with a christening outfit. "Elina," Maria began, "this is lovely. Tea will look so precious when we present her to the Lord for her baptism. You must have been up many nights working on this."

"I had to wait until Johann was asleep or the "little parrot" would have repeated what he saw."

"Elina, we want you to be our daughter's godmother," Maria shared.

"I'm very honored, your majesties."

D Marie

"My elderly father will be there, too," Albert added. "He is grateful to have lived long enough to see his first grandchild. You two are the perfect witnesses."

One day, Elina asked King Albert and Queen Maria if she could stay and help during the night. This pleased them greatly as Tea responded to Elina's tender loving care, and Tea's eyes followed Johann everywhere he went. Her first laugh came when she saw him one morning.

Johann talked baby talk with Tea, and she cooed. Playfully, he covered his eyes with his hands. Removing them, he said, "Peek-a-boo."

After Tea laughed, Johann placed his hands on the side of her baby bed. He gazed into Tea's eyes and thought, *I made her happy. I like making her happy.* And he played the game again.

Since Elina would be staying at the palace, she wouldn't be bringing food to Ari and the twins. Once again, she asked for King Albert's favor.

King Albert replied, "Ari has had a heart-breaking loss. We can help him for as long as it takes. Not only will food be taken to him, but I will personally choose a servant to prepare the food and take care of the needs of his home."

Elina raised her hand to her shoulder and bowed her head. "Thank you, Sire," she said and straightened up. "I miss being with Ari and my grandsons. Perhaps this kindness will heal his broken heart."

Afterward, Elina saw Magnus and Ivar in the town square. She quickly took Johann to the square to be with his brothers.

"How is your papa?" Elina asked.

Magnus got quiet and looked at the ground. But Ivar spoke up, "He cries, Grandma. We see him cry many times. We hear him at night in his room. What can we do?"

Journey to the Glass Hill

Elina sighed. She took a deep breath and said, "Just comfort him and pray." Elina moved closer and hugged her grandsons. "This is hard for you, too."

Magnus and Ivar looked sorrowfully at Johann. "I miss you," Johann told them.

The twins hugged their little brother. "We miss you, too."

After the twins left, Johann hid his face in his grandmother's skirt. The woolen material muffled his sobs while his chest heaved in and out. Thoughts of his father and brothers flooded his mind.

Elina returned to her home after Tea turned one, but she and Johann still came to the palace every day to help with the little girl. Every morning, one servant went to Ari's house for the day, and the other servant returned the carriage to the palace with Elina and Johann. In the evening, the carriage brought Elina and Johann home and took Ari's house servant back to the palace. The routine continued for two years.

Tea turned three shortly after Johann's sixth birthday. Her curiosity led her to investigate her surroundings. She and Johann trekked through the palace with Elina close behind them. When the weather cooperated, the two children ventured into the courtyard and explored all the paths, plants, statues, and fountains. Their friendship grew.

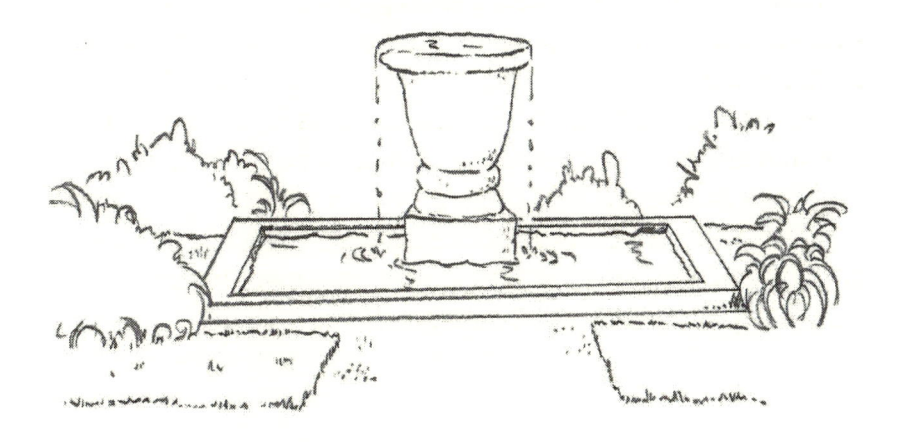

D Marie

Johann liked to play school, and Tea liked to do anything her friend wanted to do. Johann took a stick and drew letters in the dirt. Tea named them. "You are right," Johann praised her each time she gave an accurate reply. Tea's legs swung back and forth as she sat on the garden bench. Sometimes, she confused the letters, but Johann still praised her efforts. "I like the way you try, Tea. This one was tricky for me to remember, too."

Albert and Maria watched them from the window. They couldn't hear their words, but they recognized the genuine friendship the children shared. Elina stayed close by for safekeeping and quietly let the children enjoy their playtime.

"It's time for Tea's rest," Elina announced.

"May I stay a little longer in the garden?" Johann asked.

"Of course," his grandmother replied, and she took Tea inside.

Johann looked up at the nearby tree. Standing on the bench, he reached for the limb and pulled himself up into the tree. Johann enjoyed the view until he looked down, and he gasped. It was so far! His little body froze, uncertain what to do next.

The nearby guard had watched the whole event. He casually walked over and commented, "I climbed trees when I was your age. The tricky part is getting down. May I show you what I did?"

Wide-eyed Johann slowly nodded.

"Place one hand here and the other hand there. Turn your body and lean on your front side. Slowly, edge your body down while holding the limb."

Johann made it. "Thank you," he said trying to steady his wobbly legs.

"Next time," the guard replied, "have an exit strategy ready when you start a new adventure."

The young boy smiled and ran to the palace door.

Albert and Maria had observed the whole episode. "That limb needs to be removed," Albert commented.

Journey to the Glass Hill

"Perhaps," Maria began. "Or we can leave it as a reminder for Johann. He learned something today, and he overcame his obstacle."

"With a little help from the guard."

"That's true. If we were able to go through life without help, then we might put our trust in our own abilities rather than trusting God."

"The limb stays!"

Maria smiled as she patted her husband's back. *My thoughts, too.*

The day began with a constant reminder. Every morning task took longer to accomplish. Elina knew she had to make a decision, but it hurt too much to tell them. She didn't have the strength she once had. With a heavy heart, she discontinued her service to the royal family and remained at her cottage. Although she missed the royal family, keeping up with Johann filled her days.

Even though she no longer went to the palace, King Albert continued to send food for Elina's and Ari's family and a servant to help in Ari's home. The servant offered to help Elina, too. She accepted the food, but she wanted to take care of her own home and teach Johann skills that would help him in the future.

Johann learned to cook. Elina taught him how to properly use the utensils for preparing the food. He observed and mimicked his grandmother's actions, but he was never allowed to be near the fireplace unless his grandmother was there in the cooking room. Johann gained a great respect for burning wood. One day, an ember rolled out of the fireplace. Johann noticed the charred wood after the glow had diminished, and he tried to pick it up.

"Ow," he yelled, "that hurts." Tears rolled down his face as he flapped his hand back and forth.

His grandmother kissed his throbbing fingers and put his hand in a bucket of cool water. "I'll never make that mistake again," he said.

"The best lessons in life sometimes are learned through painful experiences," his grandmother shared.

"But it hurts."

"Yes, it hurts now, but only for a short time. Then, the hurt gets better." Elina kissed his forehead and started talking about Tea to distract his attention from his blistered fingers.

Walking to Christana took its toll on Elina. Losing this ability disheartened her. Under the guise of helping Johann, she accepted the palace servant's offer to take them to Christana. After she visited the weavers, she resumed making garments for her livelihood. The servant also took them to church on Sunday.

The servant asked Ari each time if he wanted to attend church. "I'm going to get Elina and Johann. Would you like to come?"

"Not today. I have a horse that needs tending. Give them my regards." Ari turned and walked away.

Ari still shied away from Johann. The twins occasionally came over to their grandmother's house, but they usually visited because they wanted something and didn't stay long. They seldom spent time with their younger brother.

Chapter 15

Always Remember

He stood guard at the window. With the target in sight, his eyes gleamed. "The carriage is here," Johann shouted. Elina took his hand, and they went outside. Johann kept staring at the front of the carriage.

"Would you like to sit next to the coachman?" Eliana asked her grandson.

"Yes!" Johann replied.

The coachman smiled and nodded his approval. After assisting his grandmother into the carriage, Johann scrambled up the side of the front wheel. Using the spokes as a ladder, he grabbed the coachman's step with his hands and raised his body up to the floorboard. Being pleased with his accomplishment, Johann grinned from ear to ear as he took his place on the coachman's seat. After the coachman took his position next to Johann, he untied the reins and commanded the horses to proceed.

The coachman raised his index finger to his lips and gave the quiet sign. Scrunching his eyebrows together, Johann tilted his head to the side as he stared at the man. The coachman smiled and motioned for Johann to move closer to his side. A smile spread across Johann's face. The uniformed driver reached one of his arms around the young boy and let the child hold the reins. Johann guided the horses down the dusty lane.

When the coachman saw the church, he looked at Johann. With a wink and a sideway tilt of his head, he let the boy know he had to let go and scoot over. Johann winked and complied with the silent instruction. Near the church entrance, the

D Marie

coachman parked the carriage and opened the door to assist his passenger.

"How was the view from the front of the carriage, Johann?" Elina asked.

"Great, Grandma. I would like to ride there again. I'll see you inside." With the graceful movements of a deer, he scampered off.

Elina and Johann looked forward to attending church and seeing their friends. The royal family also looked forward to seeing them as they missed being with Elina and Johann at the palace.

With arms opened wide, King Albert beckoned Johann to get a hug. "Come here, my godson."

After the hug, Johann checked his pocket. He found a little sweet treat. "Thank you," he said as King Albert winked at him.

Smiling brightly, Tea wrapped her arms around Johann and hugged him tightly. Holding hands, their eyes sparkled as they shared their daily activities and reminisced about their adventures in the palace garden. Johann was not alone and not without love.

One Sunday, Elina and Johann didn't come to church. *She never misses*, the minister thought. *I'll go after services to see if something is wrong.*

When Reverend Gudmund arrived, he greeted Johann. "Hello, young man. Good to see you." He reached down and rubbed Rex's head. "Hello Rex." The dog's tail became a blur as he wagged it vigorously. Elina watched and gave a deep sigh of relief.

"Johann," his grandmother called, "Rex needs some exercise. Please take him for a run." Rex provided an abundance of company for Johann and followed the young boy wherever he went. When Johann took his dog outside, she looked at the minister and said, "I have something to share."

Journey to the Glass Hill

Elina's tense voice alarmed Reverend Gudmund, and he listened somberly.

"I'm afraid my time is near." She paused. "I'm not afraid for myself. I'm afraid for Johann. Ari doesn't want him around. What will happen to him?"

"I told you the day Ari and Johanna were married that the Lord was with you, and I will be there for you, too. Elina, you are not alone," Gudmund reminded her. Elina smiled, and they talked while Johann happily played outside.

When Gudmund left, Johann waved goodbye to him and went back into the house. "Johann, come here, please," his grandmother called. "I have a gift for you." Johann walked to his grandmother's side as she took off her necklace. It was identical to the one Johanna had given King Albert and Queen Maria as a wedding present many years ago.

"Johann, put this on and place it under your shirt next to your heart," Elina said with teary eyes. Johann noticed the pendant on the necklace had a hinge, and he opened it. A cross occupied the right side, and the other half contained the words, "I love you." He closed it and placed the necklace over his neck with the locket next to his heart.

Elina continued, "Your grandfather gave this locket to me and an identical one to your mother."

D Marie

"I will treasure it forever," Johann promised. The rest of the afternoon, Johann opened and closed the locket trying to remember what his mother looked like.

The next day, Reverend Gudmund and the Court Physician came to see Elina. Johann went out to play with Rex. When the two men came outside, they looked at Johann and smiled. When they looked at each other, their smiles disappeared. They waved to Johann, and the boy waved back.

The king's servant arrived the following morning and helped Elina with the needs of her home. Ari noticed, because the servant arrived after the midday meal and explained that he had gone to Elina's house first but offered no reason for this departure in the routine. Ari sent the twins over to see what had changed. When they came back, their sad faces alarmed their father.

"What's the matter? What has happened?" Ari questioned them.

"Grandma is sick, Papa. Is she going to die, too?" Ivar's doleful eyes focused on his father seeking some type of emotional support.

"Not again!" yelled Ari. For the first time since Johanna passed away, Ari went to Elina's house. He walked in without knocking and noticed Johann sitting by his grandmother's bed.

"Leave the room!" he told the boy. When Johann had scampered out, Ari turned his head toward Elina and beheld her pale complexion. His chest tightened as he looked tenderly into her sorrowful eyes. "Elina, not you, too?"

"My time is near, Ari. You were a good son to your father, and he loved you. Johann is a good son, too. I know you love him. Ari, it's not his fault," Elina pleaded.

Ari threw his hands up in the air and walked out. Alone in her room, Elina cried out in agony. "I have to do something, but what?" Closing her eyes, she saw flowers. "The Lord will provide."

Journey to the Glass Hill

Reverend Gudmund made frequent visits. Sometimes he came with another minister. *Maybe two ministers praying are more powerful than one,* Johann guessed.

The sun shone brightly through the window when Elina reached over for Johann's hand. Looking into his eyes, she tenderly shared, "Johann, you are loved. Always keep the Lord close to your heart. Your grandfather was loving, your mother was loving, I was loving, and you are loving. The Lord is loving, too. Always remember, the Lord provides."

"Yes, Grandma, I will always remember," Johann promised.

Elina smiled, closed her eyes, and passed on. Johann laid his head on her shoulder and cried. Memories of his mother's passing now flooded his thoughts. He saw his mother sitting on the cooking room floor. His father sat behind her and held her as he cried. His brothers stood behind their father and cried. He remembered laying his head on her lap. "Blue," he said, "her dress was blue."

Chapter 16

New Life Begins

King Albert's servant frantically ran down the lane in search of Ari. When Ari saw him coming, he gasped and dropped the bucket he was carrying. Between pants for air, the servant told him about Elina.

Ari's heart pounded as he sprinted to her cottage. His life seemed to stop as he stared at Elina and contemplated her passing. Visions of his Johanna and Elina together flooded his mind. Tears stung his eyes as he thought of Elina's selfless dedication to family. Another loved one has died. Ari could bear it no longer. He closed his eyes and gritted his teeth. Regaining his hardened composure, Ari took Johann by the arm and walked him outside. "You have to live with me now. Go to the house and get inside."

Johann ran all the way down the lane. He ran past his brothers and went inside the stone house. Magnus and Ivar followed him.

"You're not going in our room!" they warned him. Johann didn't know where to go, so he went to the cooking room and sat by the fireplace ledge. The ashes on the hearth clung to his pants. As he stood up to dust the ashes off, Ari walked in and noticed Johann's dirty hands. What he wanted to say died on his lips. He turned around and left the room.

He looks like my Johanna, her hair, her eyes. I can't look at him. It's too painful, Ari agonized as he braced his back against the outside wall.

Johann saw a pile of rags and took refuge there. He laid down, curled up, and stayed there till morning.

Elina had arranged in advance for her burial. She wanted it to be simple and accomplished the day following her passing. As much as Ari didn't want to go, he did attend with his three sons. Elina was laid to rest next to her husband, the grandfather the boys had never known.

After the burial, Ari noticed the minister going into the cottage.

"Reverend," Ari blurted out, "as next of kin, I'll take over the cottage."

"You are mistaken, Ari. You are not the next of kin," the minister replied.

"I'm not, but the boys are," Ari retorted.

"You are yet mistaken," the minister replied again. "The boys are not the next of kin."

Ari gritted his teeth and his eyes narrowed as he asked one more question. "Then, who is the next of kin, Reverend?"

"Her husband. Elina and I were married. I have the paper if you would like to see it."

Anger escalated in Ari as his thoughts rumbled in his head. *I had hoped to have Magnus or Ivar live in that cottage one day, and his brother could have my house.*

"By the way, Reverend, Johann will never be in your church again," Ari said trying to soothe himself. "None of us will!" With those harsh words, Ari returned home, hollering at all the boys as they walked down the lane.

The palace servant waited in front of Ari's house. Ari greeted him and took the food. After he thanked the servant, Ari informed him that his services were no longer needed.

I don't want him snooping around here, Ari thought to himself. *Besides, I just got a new worker. I better go in and tell him what his duties are.*

Journey to the Glass Hill

Quietly, Johann sat on the hearth, thinking about his grandmother. Ari walked in and again noticed how much Johann looked like his mother. After placing the food on the table, he shook his head trying to get rid of the mental image of Johanna. He walked over to the hearth, picked up some ashes, and smeared them on Johann's face to cover up the young boy's looks.

"This is your room now. You fix the food. You clean the house. You wash the clothes. You may only call me sir and nothing else. Understood?"

"Yes, Sir," Johann managed to say. "What about my dog, Rex?"

"He's the property of the other house. He doesn't belong here."

Ari's index finger throbbed. With a puzzled look, he glanced at the fireplace and noticed a glowing ember by the extinguished ashes he had just picked up. He wiped his sooty hands on his pants and put his hurting finger in his mouth to soothe the pain as he walked out of the house. But the pain he had inflicted on Johann went much deeper.

After his father went outside, Johann looked around the cooking room. He noticed the food on the table and the utensils by the wall. Turning around, he saw that the fireplace still had some glowing embers in it.

Grandma was wise, he thought. *She taught me what to do, and I don't want to let the fire go out.*

Tears rolled down his cheeks. They made streaks through the ashes rubbed on his face. Remembering his grandmother's favorite words, "The Lord provides," Johann patted his shirt and felt the locket of love underneath. Johann got up, took a deep breath, and washed his face.

Lord, the young boy said to himself as he looked at the woodpile for the fireplace, *I don't understand why Papa is so angry, and I'm hurting, too. Please help us.*

Once more, Johann breathed deeply. This time, he felt a little better. Although his heart still ached, it seemed more bearable.

After a few moments, Ari returned with Magnus and Ivar. Johann gulped expecting another round of words. This time, Ari's anger subsided. "Magnus, fetch a pail of water."

"Do I have to?" Magnus whined. "It's Ivar's turn."

"Do as you're told. Ivar, fetch some eggs."

"Yes, Papa," Ivar replied not wanting to cross his father.

Ari turned his attention toward the last boy in the room. "Johann, show me how to boil a kettle of water."

Journey to the Glass Hill

A big knot welled up in Johann's gut. *I'm being tested. I must do my best.* He poked the embers in the fireplace and gathered them together. Rummaging through the woodpile, he selected thin sticks and slivers of wood to lay on top of the embers. The flames grew stronger. Returning to the woodpile, Johann picked up some medium sized chopped wood and added it to the fireplace.

Magnus returned with the water. "Thank you, Magnus," Johann said.

Magnus smiled but remained quiet. *I don't want Papa yelling at me for talking to Johann.*

Johann lifted the kettle to the hook in the fireplace. After he put several ladles of water in it, he swung the iron bar that held the kettle back over the fire. Turning around, he caught a glimpse of a smile on his father's face.

"Go to the larder and bring out some vegetables, peel them, and put them in the kettle," Ari ordered.

Each vegetable slowly lost its outer covering as it surrendered to Johann's knife. After the last food item joined the rest of the vegetables, Ari stood up and laid his hand on Johann's shoulder. "Always be careful with fire and sharp tools."

"I will, Sir," Johann said as he took a deep breath.

"Magnus, Ivar, we have work to do. Let's go to the barn," Ari announced.

The twins shuffled out the door behind their father. Ivar looked at Johann and nodded to him as he left. When alone, Johann slumped to the floor and quietly assured himself, *I passed the test.*

Chapter 17

The Lord Provides

Reverend Gudmund surveyed the room. He laid his bag on the table and retrieved his Bible. He only brought a few of his personal belongings. Closing his eyes, he felt the comforting warmth. Elina's prayers and love permeated the cottage.

Opening his eyes, reality took over. The thought of Ari's family not hearing the Word of God bombarded him. Trying to think of a scripture that pertained to the situation, Elina's words drifted into his mind, "The Lord provides."

He reached out to God. "Yes, Lord, You do provide. Now, I ask You to provide me a way to help. Elina wanted me to be here, so they could see Your minister, but what else can I do?"

Slowly, he trudged outside. As he sat down to rest on the porch step, a bird flew by and landed on a nearby bush. Gudmund glanced at the bird noticing its tiny feet, delicate feathers, and black eyes. The bird looked directly at him and began to sing.

How comforting it is to have one of God's creatures to share a beautiful song with me, he reflected, enjoying the bird's sweet melody.

"That's it!" Gudmund announced as he stood up, scaring the bird away. "I will share the Lord's songs from this house so the boys will hear them. I need an instrument. Where can I get one?"

The following Sunday, the townsfolk came to the church for worship. King Albert and Queen Maria always attended with their daughter. As the minister finished playing the organ,

D Marie

Tea pulled on her father's jacket and whispered in his ear. Her father smiled.

At the end of the service, King Albert talked with his wife. "This is a splendid idea," Maria replied. They waited for the church to empty, allowing them to talk to the minister alone.

"Reverend," King Albert said, "Tea was moved by your music today. She is just four years old and wants to learn to play. We have a different style of instrument with keys like the organ, two identical ones. They were wedding presents. She could practice on one of them at the palace and learn on the other one at your home. Could you teach her to play?"

Being very professional, Reverend Gudmund responded, "Yes, Sire. It would be my pleasure."

"Good," replied King Albert, "I can have the harpsichord brought to your home tomorrow if that is good for you."

"I will be there tomorrow," confirmed Gudmund.

"You can acquaint yourself with the harpsichord before Tea's lessons. What day would you like her to begin?" King Albert inquired.

Journey to the Glass Hill

"Will Saturday be a good day?" Gudmund asked.

"Yes, a very good day," responded King Albert.

"Thank you, Reverend Gudmund," said Tea smiling brightly as she gave the minister a graceful curtsy.

"You're welcome, Princess Tea," replied Reverend Gudmund. "I'm looking forward to our lessons."

After the royal family departed from the church, Gudmund closed the door and watched them through the window as they walked toward the town square. Gudmund raised his hands and proclaimed, "The Lord provides. The Lord provides. Thank You, Lord. You provided."

The following day, the harpsichord arrived at Elina's cottage. Gudmund had it placed in the front room near the windows. After the servants left, Gudmund began to play. The music drifted out the opened windows. He noticed Ari and the twins working in the field across the lane. Gudmund played louder. This time, Ari and the boys stopped working and stared at Elina's cottage. Ari rubbed his head and wondered what made the strange music. He had never heard a harpsichord before. Gradually, the melody became familiar. He had heard the song performed on the church organ. The minister played it with great gusto. Ari smiled.

"Mama loved that song, Papa." Magnus remembered.

"She would sing it as she worked in the house," Ivar added.

Ari's smile faded away. Tears welled in his eyes. It had been four years since Johanna had passed away. The pain in his heart ached as intensely as the day she died. Unable to deal with the torment, Ari turned his feelings to anger.

"I can't be listening to this. That minister is wasting the parishioners' good money on his personal pleasure. I will put an end to this now!"

Ari walked over to the cottage and knocked on the door. Gudmund was surprised but happy to see Ari. "Reverend Gudmund," Ari started.

D Marie

But before he said another word, the minister interrupted. "Good to see you, Ari. Please come in. I want to show you the king's beautiful instrument." As Ari entered the cottage, Gudmund continued. "Princess Tea will be taking lessons here on Saturdays. This is my first time playing the harpsichord. It's similar to an organ, but I don't need someone to pump the bellows."

Ari's mouth dropped open. This was not what he had envisioned. *It's the king's instrument, and Princess Tea is coming here*, he thought. "Uh, sorry to have bothered you, Reverend. Give my regards to the king." Ari hurried to the door.

Ari walked across the lane to his own property. He looked up at the sky, shook his fist, and asked, "Why do You torture me?"

When Ari returned to the field, Magnus and Ivar heard their father mutter, "It's all his fault. That boy is the cause of all my troubles."

The twins looked at each other and agreed with their father, "Yes, it's all his fault." They immediately noticed that their father smiled at this declaration, so they said it again, "It's all his fault."

Ari smiled again, walked over to Magnus and Ivar, grabbed each one in his arms, and hugged them. Ari rubbed their heads with the palm of his hands in an affectionate manner, and said, "Come on, sons, we have work to do."

As Gudmund played the music, Ari and the boys sang a different song as loud as they could. But in the house, Johann tried to remember the words of the melody being played. He couldn't tell where the music came from since the barn blocked the view of his grandmother's cottage. He imagined the sounds must be coming from there. The music comforted Johann as he reached for his heart and felt the locket under his shirt.

"Mama wore one, too," he said in a low voice. "The Lord provides." He finished sweeping the floor. "I better get busy

Journey to the Glass Hill

with the evening meal, because Father and the twins will be hungry when they come in."

Johann could only fix what he had available in the cooking room. He wished he had some of the spices his grandmother had used. Some spices accentuated the flavor of the food, and some disguised the taste. When supplies ran low, he informed his father, and Ari bought more. Johann never went to town.

When he finished his work, Johann looked around the room hoping to find something to do. The reading books rested on a nearby shelf. Since everyone had departed for town, he took a book and started to read it. With great effort, Johann persevered and sounded out the words he didn't know and began to read.

The twins always went with their father to town and looked forward to seeing the shops, the people, and the grand palace. Each time they passed the church, Ari looked the other way. Bitterness and anger still resided in his heart.

Early one morning, Magnus noticed his father smiling for a long time, and he decided to ask the difficult question, "Papa, aren't we being too harsh with Johann?"

A wild look appeared on Ivar's eyes as his eyelids spread open as far as possible. His jaw dropped, and he gasped loudly.

Ari remained calm and addressed the question. He straightened his body as he walked toward his son. Magnus felt like a grasshopper next to his towering father. Ari's narrowed eyes focused only on Magnus. The young boy quivered. An eerie look resided in his father's glare.

"Do you like living here?" Ari asked.

"Yes," Magnus responded in a whimpering voice.

"Then never say that again."

Later that day, Magnus walked into the cooking room with a chicken. "This is for the evening meal."

"Thank you, Magnus. Chicken will be great for tonight." Magnus offered a slight smile and returned to the barn.

Johann took the food, prepared it for cooking, and placed it in the kettle of water warming over the hearth fire. He added carrots, potatoes, and onions. "This will be a good meal," he said as he stirred the contents in the kettle. "I wish I could add some pepper, but the container is empty."

After the evening meal, Johann cleaned up the cooking room and sat in his corner. His work day was over, and tomorrow would be new one. *Hmm*, he pondered. *What shall I prepare for tomorrow morning?* He thought about the eggs Ivar had collected in the basket. *Eggs and salt pork will make a fine meal.* Satisfied with his mental menu, he said his prayers and went to sleep.

Johann never knew about the confrontation between Magnus and his father. Fear prevented Magnus and Ivar from repeating it. Although Magnus felt guilty, fear of his father overrode the feeling to help his younger brother. Magnus never wanted to challenge his father again.

Chapter 18

The Music Stopped

Johann walked out the door and threw a pail of dirty water into the yard. Looking up, he spotted his father leading the wagon in the field. Nearby, his brothers helped gather the remaining vegetables.

As the years went by, Ari and the twins became inseparable. Johann wondered if his father wanted to protect them or control them. Either way, he felt the difference, because his duties resided in the house.

Spending most of the day alone, Johann quickly finished his responsibilities. He looked out the window to see where Ari and the twins where. *Great luck,* he thought. *They're still in the field.* Johann opened a book. His eyes looked at the words as often as they looked out the window. His desire to read overruled Ari's directive to leave the books alone.

Teaching Johann the skill of reading did not interest Ari, but he wanted to teach Magnus and Ivar how to increase their abilities in reading and calculating numbers. Their horse and farming business depended on those skills.

Under the rulership of King Albert, the town grew. Job opportunities encouraged many families to stay. Other people came to live and work in Christana, too. This led to a larger demand for horses, and Ari's horses were the best. As more cottages were built, the empty spaces between Ari's farm and the town filled in.

"At least the land for my farm is mine. I never want neighbors close to me. They are busybodies as my father would call them," Ari reminisced aloud. It had been a long time since

D Marie

he had thought about his father. "Life was much easier then," he whispered to himself. "Back then, Johanna came into my life. Johanna, you promised not to leave me."

Ari cried out. "You didn't break your promise. God took you!" Anger, bitterness, and resentment pushed to the surface again. Ari embraced these emotions rather than letting God help him cope with his loss.

The following day, Ari sat with Magnus and Ivar teaching them mental addition. Ivar kicked Magnus and grinned. Magnus glared at his brother and slapped his arm. Johann kept his head down as he worked nearby cleaning up after the morning meal. Frustrated, Ari yelled at Magnus and Ivar when they didn't take the lessons seriously. "How many times do I have to impress upon you two? You must add these numbers in your head. When making an agreement, you must be sure you are agreeing to the correct amount. The correct amount is…?" Ari paused giving the twins a chance to respond.

One hundred nine, Johann mouthed silently.

"One hundred nine!" Ari shouted. "Lessons are over. Let's get to work."

Magnus and Ivar shrugged their shoulders and gave each other a hopeless look. Then they turned their heads toward Johann and gave him a mocking look. "You can't even add two plus two," Magnus said. They walked out the door laughing at Johann. Little did they know that Johann had added the various sums in his head nearly as fast as his father could.

After they went outside, Johann glanced out the window and watched as all three of them left for town with two extra horses. *They may be gone for a while,* Johann thought as he folded his arms, *I'll do some cleaning up to pass the time.* The side of his mouth pulled down in a slight pucker. He turned around and stared at the table and dropped his arms to his side.

Journey to the Glass Hill

The books that his father had been teaching from remained open. Johann studied them, being careful to leave the books in the same location. His father would be furious if he knew Johann had better reading and number skills than the twins who were five years older.

Johann listened to hymns filtering down the lane as he grew up. He read anything he could find. He made number problems in his head and wrote the numbers in the hearth ashes after he got an answer for comparison. His adding and subtracting abilities were very accurate. Although Johann spent most of the time alone, he never felt lonely. He kept the love of his grandmother, his mother, and God close to his heart.

He cherished the music coming down the lane. Since Johann couldn't remember the words to the melodies, he created his own lyrics to worship the Lord.

One day, the music stopped. Several days went by and still no music. Johann asked his father what happened. Ari seemed to take great pleasure in answering the boy's question and replied, "The minister has gone to meet his Maker. That should put an end to that noise he insisted on making. Since he can't teach the king's daughter anymore, I suspect that noisy instrument will be leaving, too. Good riddance!"

"Tea was there?" Johann asked.

D Marie

"Princess Tea to you," replied Ari. "Didn't you see the king's carriage over there every Saturday? Oh, I guess you can't see it, because the barn is in the way."

For the last eight years, Johann had listened and had been comforted by the hymnal music. Now that too had been taken away from him. *Reverend Gudmund is now with Mama and Grandma,* Johann imagined the three together. *He can comfort them with his beautiful music there.*

Chapter 19

New Responsibilities

Reverend Gudmund's passing brought an unexpected blessing. When Ari came out of the barn, he closed his eyes and shook his head. He opened his eyes and saw his youngest son standing in the doorway. Walking toward the house, Ari yelled, "Johann!"

"Yes, Sir."

"I have good news for you. Come here."

What's this about? Johann wondered as he approached his father.

"You are older and stronger now. How old are you?"

"Fifteen," Johann quickly replied.

"I want you to help with the horses."

"Yes, Father—I mean, Sir." Johann's eyes sparkled. The thought of being outside working with the horses thrilled him.

"Follow me." An impish smile spread across Ari's face.

Johann followed Ari all the way into the barn, but the horses were not there. "See these stalls?" Ari pointed. "They haven't been cleaned in a while. Get busy. The waste is good for growing plants, so put it all in the wagon. You can take it to the planting fields later."

Entering the barn, Johann eyed the piles of horse droppings. His heart sank, but he realized that this was a step out of the house even though it was a dirty job. After Ari finished with Johann, he searched for Magnus and Ivar. They had suddenly disappeared.

Ari found his sons near the corral. They wiped the smiles off their faces when they listened to their father. "The work in the barn will prevent Johann from preparing our meals. You two will have to cook." Magnus rolled his eyes.

"Would you rather clean out the barn?" Ari asked. "You have done it many times before."

"We'll do the cooking," Ivar volunteered. They headed for the house and grumbled all the way. Once inside, the brothers noticed that Johann had already set the food for the rest of the day on the table.

"At least we know what to cook," Magnus said.

"The trick is how do you cook it?" Ivar added.

"We're grown men," Magnus began. "How hard can this be?"

"We're going to find out," Ivar noted.

After cleaning the stalls, Johann picked up the tongue of the wagon and pulled. The wagon didn't budge. He needed horses.

Ari raised a slight pucker in the corner of his mouth at the thought of teaching Johann how to prepare for the next task. He led his son to the horse corral. Johann walked over to the horses with no intimidation at all. He had envisioned this moment for years. With great admiration, he stroked their necks, foreheads, and sides. The horses responded to his touch with acceptance.

He's just like his mother, Ari reminisced. *Why am I not surprised?* His memories stung. Ari yelled at Johann, "Come here!"

The loud noise startled one of the horses, and he reared up on his hind legs. Johann stood there. Somehow, he knew the horse would not hurt him. When the horse noticed that Johann did not show fear, the large animal calmed down and walked back to him. Submissively, the horse placed his forehead by Johann's hand, so the boy would rub his head again.

Ari watched in amazement. He couldn't control his feelings and said, "Johann, that was brave. You'll do well around these

Journey to the Glass Hill

horses." Johann tried not to show too much emotion, but he glowed on the inside.

"I'm going to teach you how to properly hitch up the team of horses to the wagon," Ari began. "These are workhorses, not pets. Treat them that way. They are trained to pull the wagon."

Johann watched how his father quickly placed the collar around the horse's neck and laid the straps on top of the horse's back. The horse patiently waited for the next requirement. Ari methodically took each strap and buckled them up. After he hitched the horse to the wagon, he pointed to the other horse and grinned. "Johann, it's your turn."

Lord help me, Johann quietly prayed. He adjusted the lopsided collar around the horse's neck. The horse eyeballed him and snorted. He laid the straps on the horse and noted the longest ones. If he tried to place a strap in the wrong area of the horse, Ari shook his head back and forth. When Johann completed the final strap, Ari nodded and pointed to the wagon. The obedient son hitched up the second horse.

Ari gave him a hearty slap on the back and demonstrated the proper technique for the next job. "Spread the manure thinly, like this. Too much will burn the growing roots of the plants. That hurts our crop production."

"Yes, Sir. I'll be careful." Johann walked to the front of the wagon near the horses' heads pretending to check their straps. He looked around to make sure his father was not within hearing range. "I will treat you with love and kindness," he whispered to the horses. "I will take care of you, and maybe you will take care of me."

Johann mounted the wagon and guided the team to the fields. A slight, warm smile appeared on Ari's face as he watched his son maneuver the rough terrain.

"Papa," yelled Ivar, "I need your help." Ari turned and headed for the barn and forgot about Johann.

Being well trained, the horses patiently waited each time when Johann stopped to spread the barn muck on the field.

D Marie

After pushing his shovel into the pile of muck on the wagon, Johann carried it to the bare dirt and sprinkled it over the soil. *This field will be ready by spring when it's time to plant*, Johann thought as he observed his work. *Maybe, I can help put the seeds in*. He continued the work for several hours, being careful to put a thin layer of the natural fertilizer on the ground.

The setting sun cast a warm glow on the field announcing the end of the daylight. Johann completed the all-day task. Working outside wore him out, but he savored the opportunity and hoped to do it again.

Pulling a wagon and standing in the midday sun exhausted the horses. Sweat covered their hair where the leather straps rubbed their bodies. Their nostrils flared as they drew in more air. Lowering their heads, their bodies indicated a need for water and rest. As Johann lead the team back to the barn, he raised his head and glanced over the stone and rail fence. For some reason, he hadn't noticed it earlier, but there it was in full view. He hadn't seen it in eight years.

"Grandma's house! It still looks the same. I wish Reverend Gudmund was still alive, but then I would still be in the house. Grandma, I miss you." He guided the horses slowly back to the barn and freed them from their harnesses. They eagerly trotted to the trough and lowered their mouths into the water to quench their thirst.

The next day, Magnus and Ivar groaned. The meals they fixed hadn't settled well with their system, and it took revenge in their guts. Thought of going to town added to their misery. Ari had customers coming and couldn't leave the farm.

"What about Johann?" Ivar moaned as he sat at the table cradling his midsection. "He can't get lost. The lane goes directly to the town square."

"All right," Ari said in exasperation, "the boy can go. Johann, come here."

"Yes, Sir," Johann replied.

Journey to the Glass Hill

"We need supplies from town. There will be too many to carry," Ari noted. "You will have to take the wagon and horses. Hitch up the team, and I'll bring the list out later."

Johann couldn't believe his ears. He would be allowed to go to town! Johann quickly went to the barn and selected the same two horses for the wagon. He carefully hitched them up, and they gave no objections to all the straps they had to wear for the task. A good night's rest had revived the once exhausted team.

Ari brought out the list for the supplies. "There are eight items on this list. I'm telling you this because you can't read. Tell the shopkeeper I'll send the coins tomorrow. Since you can't figure numbers, I can't send the coins with you today. Ask the shopkeeper to write the prices on this list. Can you count to eight?"

"Yes, Sir," Johann said as he accepted the list, trying to control his eagerness. He climbed into the wagon and happily headed for Christana. It didn't take long to pass his grandmother's house. Although it looked the same, its appearance seemed lonely. The curtains were drawn and chimney offered no smoke.

"I wonder who will live there now." The yard triggered memories of his dog. "Rex, where are you? Where did you go?"

As the wagon hit a bump in the lane, the list fell to the wagon floorboard. Johann picked up the list and started to read it. "Hmm, we need flour, sugar, salt, pepper, two large shirts, two large pairs of pants, soap, and a book about farm animals. Two large shirts and two large pairs of pants, that means there will be ten items being purchased." Johann smiled as he made up prices in his head and added up the pretend total.

Many years had passed since Johann's last visit to Christana. The lapse in time blurred his recollections, but the town seemed bigger. He noticed people dressed in fine clothing and others dressed in clothing similar to his. Some people

D Marie

dressed in very poor clothing. They looked sad and lonely. Thoughts of helping them filled his head. *What can I do? I have nothing.* Then he remembered the list. *I better take care of this immediately and get back to the farm.*

When Johann returned, Ari, who had been watching for him, asked, "Did you meet anyone?"

"Just the shopkeeper," Johann responded. "His shop was easy to find."

"Good," Ari continued. "The boys are still sick. I want you to prepare the meal tonight. If they are not well in the morning, you can take the coins to the merchant."

"Yes, Sir," Johann responded. As soon as Ari returned to the house with the supplies, Johann led the horses to the barn with the biggest smile his face could hold. *I'm getting more freedom,* he realized. *Thank You, Lord.*

Magnus and Ivar had both improved by the next day, but they didn't want to take a bumpy wagon ride. Ari looked at Johann and told him to take the coins to the merchant. As he approached the town square, he spotted two palace guards walking a dog. When the dog walked near Johann's wagon, he started barking profusely. The guards tried to hold the dog back, but he lunged toward the wagon many times. The loud noise caught King Albert's attention, and he walked to his balcony to investigate the commotion. Finally, Johann stopped his wagon, got down, and walked to the dog. The dog wagged his tail so hard the guards thought it might fall off.

"This dog likes you," one guard noticed.

"May I pet him?" asked Johann.

"If you don't, he won't settle down," the other guard replied with a big grin.

Johann extended his hand, and the dog yelped and cried. Getting closer, Johann placed both of his hands on the dog's head to comfort him. "He reminds me of a dog I once had, Rex," Johann shared.

"His name is Rex. He belongs to the king," the guard replied. Johann immediately withdrew his hands.

Johann assessed the situation. *Maybe, I should get out of here. The king may not want me petting his dog.* He looked at Rex one more time, and an inward emotion took over his actions. Johann got on his knees, gave the dog an affectionate hug, and kissed his head. Rex licked his face. Tears gathered in Johann's eyes, and he discreetly wiped them away.

"Goodbye, sirs," he finally mustered up the strength to say. "I have to leave." Johann wanted to stay with the dog. He could tell Rex liked him.

Slowly, Johann mounted the wagon and continued to the merchant's shop with the coins. At the same time, King Albert watched from his balcony. With a deep sigh and a smile, he said, "The Lord provides. That's Johann, my godson, leading the wagon."

Chapter 20

The Word Is Found

Johann returned quickly from town. Ari noticed, and he did something unexpected. He led Johann to the barn and taught him how to saddle a horse. After the horse was saddled, Ari had Johann saddle two more horses. When Johann was finished, Ari called for the twins, "Magnus, Ivar, come here."

Both came out of the house with their new shirts and pants on. As they walked by Johann, they dropped their old clothes at his feet. "These are yours," the two mocked Johann. "We wear men's clothes now."

Johann recognized the outfits. He had brought them back from town the day before. Magnus and Ivar had turned twenty, and Ari took them to town to celebrate their birthday. His twin sons were men.

With glinting eyes of anger, Johann watched as his father and brothers rode their horses until they were out of sight. "I am so tired of this. It's unfair. I never get included. I try so hard to please my father, and what does it get me? More pain. I should leave this place and try to get a job in town. The shopkeeper might hire me. At least he's nice to me."

With the three of them gone for the evening, Johann went to his grandmother's cottage kicking the dirt as he walked. Peering through the windows, he saw it still had the same furniture inside. "Reverend Gudmund didn't change a thing." He walked to the backyard and stood next to his grandparents' graves. Tears flowed as he remembered the love he and his grandmother had shared together. Suddenly, Johann remembered his mother's grave. It was off limits to him. "I don't care if I get caught," he muttered, running to his own yard.

As Johann got closer to the grave site, his steps shrank. It took great effort to approach where she was laid. He hadn't been there since the day she was buried. He closed his eyes and tried to remember what his mother looked like. "Blue. I remember blue. Her dress was blue. I wonder if her dresses are still in her room? Everyone is gone. I'm going to look."

Johann contemplated what he might find in his father's room. He never had to clean it or his brothers' room. None of them wanted him touching their personal things. Both bedroom doors remained shut concealing their contents.

Slowly, Johann opened the door and walked into his father's room. He noticed it looked clean, but it had a faint stale, earthy odor. The closed curtains made the light dim inside the room. An uncomfortable feeling gnawed at him.

As he looked around the room, Johann spoke out loud, "Where would Mama's things be?" In a corner, he noticed a chest. Nothing was on it except a yellow flower. It looked completely dried and fragile. With precise handling, Johann picked up the flower and laid it on the floor. He lifted the lid of the chest and saw a blue dress—the dress she had worn when Johann had laid his head on his mother's lap for the last time.

Under the dress, he found a book. "What kind of book is this?" He remembered how his mother would teach his brothers how to read. A smile appeared on his face as memories of his mother became very vivid. Johann opened the book and started to read. He saw the word Psalms at the top of the page.

Journey to the Glass Hill

"I remember Psalms. This is the Lord's Book." Johann lifted his head and gritted his teeth. Pent up emotions filled his heart as his breathing became rapid. He could hold it in no longer and prayed with anger, "Jesus, what have I done wrong? My mother is gone. My grandmother is gone. My father doesn't like me. My brothers tease me. I don't see the purpose of these circumstances. Help me to understand." He closed the Bible and reopened it. The pages fell open to the second chapter of Luke. His eyes focused on one word, Jesus. Johann began to read the following verses.

Jesus was twelve years of age when he stayed behind instead of going with His family group and friends. He had gone to the Lord's temple to converse with the teachers. His worried mother and father found their child and scolded Him. Jesus returned to Nazareth with His parents and was submissive and obedient to them. Johann lowered his head. "Jesus, You were obedient to your parents. Help me to be obedient and get through this. Help me to be like You."

Johann looked down at his mother's dress. With great anguish, he lifted the blue dress up to his face and caressed it. Reluctantly, he laid it back in the chest. After he closed the lid, he replaced the flower in the same location it had been before. Turning around, he realized that he had forgotten to replace the Bible. Johann's ears perked up. Clopping hoofs and loud neighing announced the arrival of the horse sellers.

D Marie

A look of dread appeared on Johann's face. His heart raced. He grabbed the Book and left the room. After closing his father's door, he hid the Book in the cooking room under the rags used for cleaning. *They'll never look here*, he thought. Afterward, he ran outside.

"May I take the horses back to the barn for you?" Johann asked.

Ari looked at the boy, then momentarily looked at Magnus and Ivar. Returning his attention to Johann, Ari said, "Yes, and curry the horses' backs after you remove their saddles. It's good for their skin."

"Yes, Sir, I will."

As Ari walked to the house with the twins, he wondered what was going on. *Something is different with that boy*, he thought. *What could it be?* He shrugged and turned to his twins. "Boys, I mean men, wasn't that a great ride?"

"Yes, Papa, it was a great ride."

As Johann guided the horses to the barn, he reflected on finding the Bible. *Should I put it back?* he wondered. *If I keep the Book out, I can read about God.*

The teenage boy prayed for guidance. Every time he thought about reading the Book, he smiled and felt wonderful. Every time he thought about returning the Book, he felt sad and miserable.

Johann looked up and said, "Lord, Your Word is the spiritual food I need in my life. Thank You. I'll keep the Bible, read Your Word, and grow in my relationship with You, Jesus. Forgive me for getting angry. I don't know Your will and plan for my life, but I will trust in You. You do provide."

Chapter 21

Honor Is Given

King Albert took a deep breath and bowed his head for prayer. Gazing at his folded hands, he asked for strength for today's duty, public hearings. "Lord be with me that I may know and do Your will. Amen."

The townsfolk respected their king for his wisdom. Albert encouraged Christanans to settle their own differences, but when that was impossible, he held court and listened to their disputes. Afterward, he excused himself to go to a quiet room and consider the true problem. If it was very apparent, he gave an immediate ruling. If not, he took more time to think and investigate the situation to come to a just decision. Although he knew it was impossible to please both parties involved, King Albert held truth and justice as the standard to balance his decisions. In most cases, the opposing people agreed with his ruling and left his court on amicable terms.

The week Reverend Gudmund passed away presented a heavy workload for Albert. When he saw his daughter coming into the court room, he knew it had to be very important. He beckoned her to join him and sit by his side. Tea patiently listened to the people with their comments and complaints as each person had their turn to petition the king. She remained seated as her father left the room to consider his evaluation of the testimony and his decision for the outcome. Between petitioners, Tea shared her reason for coming to the court room.

"Father," she began, "this Sunday will be the first Sunday without Reverend Gudmund. The neighboring minister presided over the funeral, but he couldn't stay. When the

D Marie

parishioners come for worship on Sunday, there will be no minister to lead them."

King Albert leaned sideways in his chair and marveled at his daughter's observation. *She is developing into a sovereign that is concerned for her subjects*, he thought as his chest puffed out a little.

"What do you suggest we do?" he replied.

"Reverend Gudmund always played the organ, and there is no one that can play the organ in Christana. I can play the harpsichord. If I practice every day, I could play the organ on Sunday," Tea shared.

Tears welled in his eyes. His daughter had thought about this problem and had a solution.

"If I may suggest," she said, pausing briefly to gather her thoughts, "perhaps you can lead the church in a time of reflection of Reverend Gudmund's life with us."

The music and sermon will continue, thought the king. *My little girl is only twelve, but she is already demonstrating wisdom and understanding. That is straight out of Proverbs. King Solomon himself would be proud of her.*

"Tea, this is a wonderful plan. Select your hymns, and I will work on the reflections."

For the rest of the afternoon, King Albert labored to give his full attention to his petitioners. Trying to keep his mind focused, he asked each group to talk to each other one more time before they came before him. As he allowed the groups time to talk, Albert lowered his head and quietly prayed, "Lord, give me wisdom for what to say on Sunday." When he lifted his head, all the petitioners were gone.

"They all shook hands and left, Your Majesty," the guard informed him.

"The Lord provides," Albert said with a smile on his face. He retired to his private quarters to compose his sermon. Thoughts of his father drifted into his mind. Albert

Journey to the Glass Hill

remembered the memorial service Reverend Gudmund gave when his elderly father had passed away.

"Reverend Gudmund, I am getting a glimpse of how difficult some of your duties were for you," Albert confessed in a low voice. "I pray to You, Lord, that I can offer the same honor for Reverend Gudmund as he gave honor to my father when he passed away."

When Sunday arrived, most of the worshipers thought it would be a quiet day. They came prepared to pray for Reverend Gudmund and for his replacement. To their surprise, King Albert waited at the church door to greet everyone. Tea sat by her mother. After everyone settled down, Tea walked over to the organ. A young boy followed her. After the boy pumped the bellows on the organ, he nodded to Tea.

D Marie

She played a familiar hymn. The people sat in quiet awe for the first verse. When the second verse started, everyone rose to their feet. Some of them managed to offer their voices in song to worship God. Some of the worshipers could only listen and think about the words. Grief had a profound effect on the people in the pews. No one was smiling. Tea noticed and only played one hymn.

After finishing the song, Tea nodded toward her father and returned to her pew. The young boy also returned to his seat. King Albert had remained in the back of the church. He took a deep breath and walked down the aisle, stood in front of the church, and bowed before the Holy Bible laying on the altar. After he offered a quiet prayer, King Albert rose and faced the parishioners.

"Today, I am not your king, but your servant," Albert confessed. "When Princess Tea suggested I speak to you today, I was overwhelmed. I prayed and asked the Lord for guidance.

"Reverend Gudmund was the Lord's servant. He served each one of us in this town. He put our needs ahead of his own. He was here the day I returned to Christana with my betrothed, Maria. He joined our hearts and souls in marriage. He was a source of encouragement as we waited many years for a child. He baptized the most precious little girl in our lives, Tea. All of us have wonderful memories of Reverend Gudmund. He played the organ with such gusto that I thought his fingers must belong to the Lord's angels. His sermons always found a way to minister to everyone to help them with their spiritual walk and understanding of God's Word. Whatever the need was, he was there to help. Finding a replacement will be difficult. But, we don't want to just replace Reverend Gudmund, we want to build on what he has started in our town. Let's all bow our heads in prayer."

Albert paused and took another deep breath. After he regained his composure, he continued. "Lord, thank You for Reverend Gudmund. Our hearts are grieving, and we miss him.

Journey to the Glass Hill

We ask for Your Holy Spirit to comfort us during our time of sorrow. We ask You for favor and to send us a minister who will be a part of our family of Christana and shepherd Your flock. In Jesus' Name, we pray. Amen."

The following month, a new minister came to Christana. He was an older man with a constant smile and an amiable presence about him. It didn't take long for Lars to settle in and proceed with his calling as the Lord's servant. Although the townsfolk were supposed to make Lars feel welcomed, Lars was the one with an overwhelming desire to put his flock at ease. Everyone who met him felt assured that Lars would continue to build on what Reverend Gudmund begun.

Chapter 22

Patience

Magnus pursed his lips and shook his head. Ari looked at Ivar who made the same response. Both brothers pointed to the house. They both felt they had more important things to do than to run errands in town.

Reluctantly, Ari allowed Johann to take over this responsibility of fetching supplies. However, Magnus and Ivar did enjoy going to town in the evening. That's when the inns would attract those who wanted to enjoy a meal that wasn't prepared at home. Their favorite innkeeper offered traditional foods as well as some recipes the new citizens brought from their native countries.

Periodically, a language barrier made understanding each other difficult. Eventually, the newcomers acclimated to the language of Christana. Some of the townsfolk learned the new languages and offered their services as interpreters. Christana grew and attracted many new visitors. This brought new trade and commerce opportunities. It also brought an unwelcome circumstance.

One day, a traveler stayed at the inn. There was nothing alarming about the man when he checked in, but the next day he ran a high fever and his body ached. The innkeeper sent word to King Albert asking to have him examined by a physician.

The Court Physician came quickly. After his examination, he gave the ailing man an herbal drink for the pain. The physician stood back to contemplate the situation. He rubbed his fingers across his forehead as he pondered his next move

D Marie

while his patient fell asleep. He left the room and searched for the innkeeper.

"I can't take a chance; I must quarantine your inn," the physician said. "No one can leave or enter." After giving the innkeeper instructions for the stricken man, he returned to the palace and sequestered himself to his personal living quarters.

Rumors of the plague returning filtered through the town. The older residents remembered the deadly disease. Fear of getting the plague invaded their thoughts. No one gathered in the town square. The brave souls who did ventured to the streets wrapped cloths over their mouths as a precaution.

King Albert and Queen Maria agonized over the ill traveler. Did he have the plague? They both prayed. Albert consulted with his counselors to set up a plan of action to contain the

Journey to the Glass Hill

disease if necessary. Afterward, another decision weighed on Albert's mind.

"Should we send Tea away or keep her here?" Albert asked Maria. "The sadness and grief I felt when my mother died of the plague was awful. I longed to be with my father after I was sent away from Christana, away from the plague." Albert lowered his head and took a deep breath.

"Albert," Maria began, "this is not an easy decision, but if we choose to keep Tea in Christana, we could keep her in the palace until the man in the inn recovers. Hopefully, no one else will become ill."

"Keeping Tea here may give the people some reassurance for their own families," Albert added. "She will stay in Christana."

One week went by, and no one else in the inn became sick. One more week went by, and the traveler at the inn started to recover. After the third week, the Court Physician returned to the inn. After examining the man and the other occupants, the physician lifted the quarantine and returned to his duties.

Still, the innkeeper received instructions to remove all the bedding material and burn it outside the town. The inn had to be cleansed from top to bottom. The innkeeper didn't perceive this as a problem. He needed to encourage his customers to return.

The innkeeper went beyond these requirements. He bought new bedding to replace the discarded ones and new dishes for serving food. Desiring to redecorate the interior, he had new tables and chairs made. Flower boxes were placed under the windows to give the outside a pleasant appearance. It was a costly adventure, but he theorized, "It takes money to make money."

After the renovations, the inn's business picked up significantly. A nearby innkeeper noticed as his business diminished. Christanans, who normally ate at home, came out

D Marie

of curiosity to see the renovations and have a meal. The prosperity of the inn amazed the other shopkeepers.

"Hmm," said the owner of the food shop, "I wonder if I should do some renovations myself?" He went to the innkeeper to find out who he had hired to do the work.

"The gentleman who was ill did all of the carpentry," the innkeeper replied. "Being confined with Hans for three weeks gave us many opportunities to talk. He informed me of his skills and what he had accomplished in other villages. Hans is still in Christana living here at my inn."

Grieving for the ill traveler and his flock, Reverend Lars prayed constantly. During the quarantine at the inn, the townsfolk avoided going to worship at the church. Even the king and queen refrained from attending. Once the quarantine was lifted, the parishioners and the royal family returned. Reverend Lars' eyes brightened to see the sanctuary full of people. His smile stretched from ear to ear, and he quietly gave thanks to the Lord for the health and prosperity of Christana.

When Hans sat in the church pew, no one would sit by him, but when the innkeeper came in, he sat so close to the carpenter that it made the man feel squashed. He gave the innkeeper an odd look and moved over.

Magnus and Ivar didn't attend church, but they were curious about the inn's renovations and went there for a meal with their father. King Albert walked by and noticed the three men having a great time at the inn. He searched for Johann, but he was not with them.

Albert often thought of his godson. *I wonder if Johann can still read? I'll devise a plan to find out.*

Knowing Johann normally came to town on the day after Sunday, King Albert requested the palace guard to stand in the square with a rolled parchment. When he saw Johann approaching, the guard walked to the public announcement

Journey to the Glass Hill

board. He waved at Johann and asked for assistance. Johann stopped the horses and obliged the guard. He held the parchment in place while the guard nailed it. As the guard swung his hammer, Johann looked at the words. Then, he looked at the guard.

"Sir, if you need this, we have plenty. I will ask my father if he is willing to sell it," Johann offered.

"Excellent," replied the guard, "I will make sure the proper person is informed."

Once Johann rode out of sight, the guard removed the parchment, rolled it up, and returned to the palace to report to King Albert.

"Yes, Your Majesty, he has plenty," said the guard as he handed the parchment to the king, "but he wants to ask his father first."

As the guard walked away, King Albert unrolled the parchment and read it to himself:

Wanted
Chicken Manure for the Royal Garden.
Inform the palace guard if you have some to sell.

Albert smiled. "Johann can still read."

Johann returned home to tell his father about the needs of the palace. Ari laughed.

"Buy chicken manure?" he asked. "For five coins, the palace can have it delivered and spread on the ground. Anything you make after that is yours."

"Thank you, Sir," Johann said reflecting on the amazing opportunity to keep some of the coins. The next morning, Johann headed for the barnyard when Ari yelled at him, "You will be busy all day with that smelly muck. The twins and I will go to the inn for the evening meal tonight."

No cooking today, Johann thought. *I better take something with me to eat later.*

D Marie

Johann toiled most of the morning. Fortunately, a good layer of the manure covered the ground. The chicken coop area needed to be cleaned anyway. Unlike the barn stalls, the chicken yard was outside. Johann parked the wagon close to the fence for easier loading, but the pungent smell made the work challenging for his nose.

After the wagon was loaded, he hitched up the horses and slowly guided them to town. Once he arrived at the palace, the guards directed him to the garden area where he would unload the wagon. The soil had been turned over and prepared for the natural fertilizer. Johann used caution.

"This muck can hurt or even kill plants instead of help them," he reminded himself. "I have to thinly spread it on the soil."

Sweat beaded up on Johann's face as he toiled in the heat of the day. He paused to wipe his brow and noticed some things in the garden that looked familiar…as if he had been here before. After completing the work, Johann placed his shovel in the wagon as the servant arrived to escort him to the palace entrance. The servant discretely tried to cover his nose with a handkerchief as he walked next to the wagon.

Another servant came out with a piece of parchment which he read to Johann, "Four coins for the manure, two coins for delivery, and three coins for spreading, that is…" The servant paused. "Pardon me. I forgot to write a total." The servant purposely stalled to add the numbers in his head while looking at them on the parchment.

Johann waited for a while then he said, "Nine."

"Yes, yes, it is," the servant agreed. He counted out the coins from the bag fastened to his belt and gave them to Johann.

"Thank you, Sir," Johann said. "If you need more, please let us know." He guided the horses back to the farm, thankful for his good fortune.

Journey to the Glass Hill

From the palace balcony, King Albert smiled when he heard the servant and Johann discussing the coin total. "Johann can add numbers in his head," Albert noted. "I think we'll need more manure in the future."

Chapter 23

The Visitor

Ari watched his son pick up the wooden handle. The novice adjusted his grip and raised the tool over his head. Thoughts of his father's advice rumbled in his mind. *Always be careful with sharp tools.* The ax came downward with a forceful blow, breaking the standing log into two pieces.

Ari smiled. He walked over to Johann and slapped him on the back. "Well done. Chopping wood is your responsibly now."

"Thank you. I'll do my best, Sir." Holding the ax in one hand, Johann concealed his free hand by his side until it stopped trembling. He had passed another test.

Ari and the twins went to neighboring villages to look for future business prospects. Wanting to control Johann's whereabouts during their trip, his father forbade him from leaving the farm.

Peering out the window, Johann waited until they were out of sight. He retrieved his mother's Bible and let go a deep sigh as he thought about the comfort the Word gave him. New knowledge waited for him on the pages. He envisioned King David's tribulations and triumphs in the Book of Psalms. He gleaned wisdom from Proverbs for his own goals in life. The teenaged boy reflected on how the people in the Bible persevered during their time of need. The Lord answered their prayers, but sometimes the provision took a while to happen.

D Marie

"What will I do when I become a man and leave this farm?" Johann spoke aloud. "Would Father even let me go? If I leave, who would do the chores I do now?" Leaning away from the table, he laughed at the thought of Magnus cooking and Ivar washing clothes.

The words of his grandmother came drifting back, "The Lord provides." Johann embraced those words. "Whatever I do, I will do it with the help of the Lord. I put my trust in Him." As Johann thumbed through the pages, he paused in the Gospels (Matthew, Mark, Luke, and Johann) and read the verses. "Some of these words are difficult to understand. I wish I had someone to explain them to me."

One evening while Johann read the Bible, he heard a knock at the door. *Maybe it's someone needing a horse*, he thought. When he opened the door, he saw a very poor peasant dressed in tattered and patched clothing. Johann didn't know many people in town, and he had never seen this person before.

"May I help you?" Johann asked politely.

"If I have favor with you, may I have something to eat? It has been awhile since I have had food," replied the peasant. "Maybe, I can do some work for you in the barn or field to repay you?"

"I would like to give you some food. Please sit down here on the porch, and I will bring something for you to eat," responded Johann. Quickly, he ladled some stew from the kettle into a bowl and picked up some bread. Johann returned with a clean cloth, laid it next to the peasant, and served him a hot meal. The peasant slowly ate the food, keeping his face turned away from Johann.

Perhaps he is embarrassed to have to ask for food, Johann thought.

Journey to the Glass Hill

"What can I do in return for your kindness, young man?" the peasant asked.

"Please, accept this as my humble gift," Johann replied. "Someday, you may return the favor to someone else. That will be payment for me." Johann took three coins from his pocket and gave them to the poor man.

The peasant looked at the gift in Johann's hands and asked, "Why are you giving me these coins?"

"I am a poor person, too, and a generous man shared these coins with me. It must have made him feel very good inside, because that is how I feel right now. Please take them."

"Thank you. May the Lord bless you. You are a kind person." The peasant tucked the coins in his pocket and walked away.

The peasant never returned. Johann often wondered about him and prayed for the man to be in good health, warm, and have plenty to eat.

The following afternoon, his father and brothers returned from their journey without the extra horses. Johann saw them as he walked to the barn. While Ari remained on his horse, he asked, "What's for the evening meal?"

"I didn't know when you were returning. I'm sorry, I don't have any food prepared."

D Marie

Ari's eyebrows lowered to a frown. "Nothing? We have been traveling a great distance, and we are hungry. Come on, sons. Let's go to the inn. They always have food ready."

"Let's go, Papa," affirmed Magus and Ivar.

When Ari used the word, sons, Johann knew he was not referring to him. Ari, Magnus, and Ivar went to the inn, and Johann went back inside to the cooking area. When he walked in, he noticed the Bible laying on the table. His heart raced. *If Father saw this*, Johann thought, *he would have been angrier than he is right now. I must be more careful.*

Johann thought about food and feeding people. He reminisced about the peasant who had come the day before. His eyes glanced down at the Bible. The words seemed to jump off the page at him:

Simon, son of Johann, do you love me?
Feed my lambs. Feed my sheep.

"That's it!" Johann exclaimed. "Yes, Lord, I love You. I was given an opportunity to feed Your people, and I was obedient. Thank You for teaching me."

Johann tidied up the house one more time. He placed the Bible under the rag pile next to his sleeping area. Before he fell asleep, he said his prayers, "Thank You, Lord, for what I have. I ask for Your hand to be upon me and to continually guide me. In Your Name, I pray. Amen."

Chapter 24

Business Is Good

Ari and the twins looked around the unfamiliar path as they traveled further away from Christana. An occasional farm house dotted the landscape. The concerned looks on their faces soon disappeared when they entered the unknown village. Happy faces greeted them.

Word spread quickly that the horse sellers had arrived. Their reputation of quality horses proceeded them, and they sold all the extra horses. They returned to the farm with a list for future purchases.

Ari shared the profits with Magnus and Ivar. He wanted his sons to be able to afford a living for themselves. *Maybe they will build their homes by me when the time comes to get married*, Ari imagined and he smiled broadly. *I could be a grandfather someday. Then, I can take life easier.*

Thoughts of Elina's house came to mind. *The new minister must want to live closer to the church. Maybe that's why he didn't take up residence in Elina's old cottage. I wonder who will move in there, or for that matter, who owns it now since Gudmund has passed away? Someday, I'll find out.* His train of thought was interrupted.

"Food is ready," Johann yelled.

Ascending from the bowls, a warm mist of steam greeted Ari, Magnus, and Ivar. While they enjoyed their meal, Johann waited on them. Afterward, Ari and the twins retired to the adjoining room, and Johann cleaned up the cooking room. Occasionally, Ari watched Johann from the other room and noticed his changed appearance.

What am I going to do with him when he is fully matured? Ari wondered. *He's almost as tall as I am and has a muscular build. I may not be able to order him around much longer.*

Something crashed on the floor. "Sorry," yelled Johann.

Maybe, the boy won't be a problem after all. He smiled and returned his attention to his other sons.

"How many horses should we take next time?" questioned Magnus. "We always sell every horse."

"Perhaps we should purchase more land around us," suggested Ivar. "Then we would have more grazing fields and could expand the business."

That idea intrigued Ari. "I'll go to the church and inquire of the minister about the ownership of Elina's old cottage and land. Perhaps we can purchase that land. It should be ours anyway."

The following morning, Ari went to town alone. After tying his horse to the rail, he took a deep breath and entered the church. It had been many years since he'd been in the Lord's house, and he felt uncomfortable. Something inside of him wanted to get out of there, but Ari was on a mission and dismissed the feeling. He followed the sound of a pounding noise and found the minister adding a support board on a pew.

"Let me hold that for you," Ari offered.

"Thank you," replied the minister. "It's difficult to hold the board and swing the hammer at the same time."

Ari hoped his help would get him on the minister's good side when he asked about Elina's cottage. "Reverend, I notice you never use the cottage near my farm."

"You are Ari, correct?"

"Yes, uh, excuse me for not introducing myself when you came to our town," Ari replied as he sheepishly winced his face and cast his eyes toward the floor.

"Don't be concerned, Ari" the minister offered, trying to put him at ease. "It has taken me a while to remember everyone's name. I may have met you and have forgotten. My name is Lars."

"Pleased to meet you, Reverend Lars."

"Pleased to meet you, Ari. I hear you have a gift with horses. Someday, I would like to see your farm."

"Speaking of farms," Ari interjected, "I notice you never use the cottage where Reverend Gudmund lived."

"Yes, it is a wonderful cottage, but I am not the owner."

"Is the church the owner?"

"The church isn't the owner either."

"I'm confused," said Ari, puzzled. "Who owns that property?"

"King Albert does," replied Lars. "Reverend Gudmund lived there until he passed away. There was a provision in the title for the king to take possession when that happened. It was Elina's way of repaying the king for saving her daughter during her pregnancies. Johanna was her name. Did you know her?"

Life drained from Ari's face.

"Did I say something wrong?" asked Lars.

Ari gave a deep sigh. In a quiet voice, he replied, "Johanna was my wife. She died many years ago. I am sorry to have bothered you, Reverend."

Ari left the church and returned home. When the twins saw him, they instantly knew something was wrong and stayed inside the house. It was Johann who went out and offered to take his horse to the barn. Ari dismounted, looked at Johann, and spoke, "Johann, I can still see a little of your mother's features in your face. She was the love of my life. I'm going inside now. Thank you for taking care of my horse."

D Marie

Johann could never remember his father talking kindly to him. He treasured that moment. *There is still hope*, Johann believed. With a deep sigh that raised his chest, Johann walked the horse to the barn talking affectionately to the large steed and rubbing his neck.

Chapter 25

A Memorable Day

Johann's eyes sparkled. He wondered if his father would acknowledge his coming of age like his older brothers. His twentieth birthday came, but nothing happened. *Perhaps, he doesn't remember*, Johann surmised. Determined to make the best of his day, he changed his thought pattern. *I pray for a memorable event to remember this day of my life.*

"Johann!" Ari yelled.

"Yes, Sir," Johann replied.

"I need some things from town," Ari said. "Look at this list. It would have been better if you'd learned to read, but too late for that. Find someone who can read and go to the different shops for the supplies we need. Here are the coins. There should be plenty. Act like you can count so I am not overcharged. Come back quickly. We have several horses to deliver, and we're leaving tomorrow."

Johann hitched up the wagon and went to town. He passed his grandmother's cottage. No one had lived there since Reverend Gudmund passed away, but the cottage remained in pristine condition. *It amazes me that I never see anyone there. Perhaps the workers come when I'm in the house. That barn is always in the way.*

When Johann reached the town square, he noticed an unusual energy in the townspeople. Excitement filled the air. *What is going on?* he wondered. Johann continued to proceed to the food shopkeeper.

"I better look at that list," Johann muttered. "Hmm, I need to go to the blacksmith, the leather tanner, and the food shopkeeper."

Johann stopped his wagon in front of the shopkeeper.

"Good morning, Johann!" the shopkeeper greeted him. "How are you today?"

"Good morning to you, Sir. I'm fine, thank you."

"Have you heard the rumor going around?" the shopkeeper asked.

"I haven't. What is it?"

"Princess Tea is seventeen years old. Usually when a princess is eighteen, she marries. Some people think that there will be some type of announcement coming soon."

"Why is everyone excited about that?"

"Because the one she marries will live in the palace and help rule the kingdom someday. Maybe she will pick someone from Christana!"

"How will her future husband be chosen?" Johann inquired.

"That's a good question," the shopkeeper replied. "If I could choose someone, I would choose you."

"Why me? I am a lowly person and certainly not worthy of that honor or privilege."

"Johann, I have known you for many years. The Lord's Hand is on you." Another customer walked in, and the shopkeeper quickly filled Johann's order.

As Johann walked out of the door, the shopkeeper smiled and said, "God bless you, Johann."

"God bless you, too," Johann replied.

Johann went to the other shops to get the supplies needed for his father's journey. He carefully watched the coins being counted so his father paid the required amount.

Ari offered a faint smile as he examined Johann's work. His son had acquired the correct supplies and had spent the correct number of coins according to the tally.

Journey to the Glass Hill

"Johann," Ari said, "the twins and I will be gone for a few weeks. You may go to town when you need supplies. Ask the shopkeeper to write a list of the items you bought. I am giving you ten coins now, and I want a full report of everything while we're gone. I feel that something is going to happen. Tell me when we get back."

"Yes, Sir," Johann replied.

"Make sure the animals are properly fed and all of your chores are finished," the twins chimed in.

"Yes," Johann replied, "I will take care of everything."

"Come on, sons!" Ari said with enthusiasm. "We have a long ride ahead of us." The three of them gathered the horses to be sold and departed.

Closing his eyes, Ari gritted his teeth. "I forgot something." He turned his horse around and went back. "Johann, since we are going to be away for a long time, you will have to continue exercising the remaining haltered horses. You have seen Magnus and Ivar do it many times. I am trusting you to do it correctly. We will do the final training when we get back."

"Yes, Sir," replied Johann.

After Ari, Magnus, and Ivar rode away with the group of horses and were out of sight, Johann shouted, "I get to walk the horses!" In a slightly lower voice, he said, "I have never been allowed to do this. Perhaps this will be the memorable event in my life."

Johann ran to the barn and pasture to count the horses. Excluding the work horses, he counted thirty, but only ten horses wore halters. Johann started to figure the time for walking each horse in his head. "About two horses per hour. Hmm, at least five hours of walking horses. Not much free time after my other chores are finished. I better get busy."

As Johann finished counting, the newest addition to the farm neighed in the distance. Ari had brought him back during one of his horse deliveries. This horse stood out from among the others. His black coat glistened in the sunlight, highlighting his sleek lines. When he shook his head, his long mane flowed in the air revealing a patch of white hair on his forehead. The high-strung stallion demonstrated his spirited nature by stomping the ground in defiance when people came near him. Johann knew he wasn't to be walked for future training. The stallion was a permanent resident.

Gathering the horses for walking required very little effort. Johann poured fresh grain in the troughs and the horses willingly entered the corral. He sectioned off the haltered ones and let the other horses return to the open pasture.

Johann intuitively knew the importance of developing a good rapport with the horses. He saw his brothers' technique many times. One by one, he fastened the lead rope to the halter. He rubbed and patted each horse on their left and right sides. Johann talked calmly but firmly to the horses. Some of the horses flinched at his initial touch, but they submitted and gave the new trainer their respect.

The black stallion stood close to the rails and watched. Every time Johann approached another horse for walking, the stallion snorted and intensely stared at him. The last horse to be exercised walked toward the rail by the stallion. Johann gulped and followed him. The stallion neighed loudly and stomped his front legs. Startled, Johann fell backward. He stood up and dusted off his pants. Although his pride was hurt, he buried his emotions and glared at the stallion. In return, the stallion exhaled out of his nose, relaxed, and walked away.

Near the corral, an area had been sectioned off where the horses underwent their workout. Since the horses were accustomed to the obstacles, their confidence had already been established. Johann did not have the more difficult job of introducing and training a horse to the expectations of the course. Although they already knew what to do, the horses still needed to be walked through each hurdle to keep them from regressing in their skill level.

Journey to the Glass Hill

Johann's father created the obstacle course many years ago and added more features as time went by. In the beginning of his horse training, Ari wanted to get the horse to accept the saddle and rider. But, he discovered through trial and error that there was more to be learned by the trainer and by the horse.

Ari favored going left when he worked with a horse. One day, he started the course backward and led off to the right. The horse behaved as if it was his first time on the course and hesitated attempting every obstacle. At first, Ari was puzzled. He quickly realized that the horse must have equal training for both sides of the body and in both directions. After that day, his horses did much better on and off the course. He only shared this knowledge with Magnus and Ivar.

Johann had learned the method by observing his father and brothers and listening to them talk at meal time. Leading the horses from their left and right sides was important. Both sides of the horses' visual fields and their thought process needed to be trained.

To keep the activity from becoming routine, Johann changed the order of the exercises. One activity had three logs laid down parallel to each other with a space between each log. The horse had to carefully maneuver all four legs at the same time to walk through that obstacle.

Some of the areas had hurdles to overcome. Short wooden fences, a ditch, and a hedge of bushes required a small jump to proceed. The horses had to know where their feet were all the time. One area contained large, smooth stones that were recessed in the ground. This challenged every horse. The noise their hoofs made on the hard surface and the unevenness of the stones bothered them. This obstacle required patience. After a while, the horses would enter that area with no resistance or objections.

Johann wondered who was getting the most exercise, the horse or him, as he had to run to keep up with the large animal on parts of the course. At the end of the walk, he led the horses

D Marie

to a different area to enjoy another portion of grain and return to the pasture.

All the obstacles on the course had a purpose. Running around in the pasture did not prepare the horses for what they would encounter in the real world. Paths, paved streets, and the woods all offered challenges the horses had to overcome.

Later that evening, Johann reflected on his first day working with the horses. Every time he tried to sit down, he popped up off his chair and paced the floor. The young man's eyes sparkled, and a wide smile remained permanently glued on his face for hours.

His thoughts drifted to the exercise course and how the horses met each obstacle with confidence. He raised his head and smiled. Wisdom and understanding came to him. "In the beginning, the horses were hesitant about the course and avoided the obstacles. Now that they're familiar with it, the horses are trusting and graceful in their approach. Exactly like people." Johann mentally surveyed the field in his mind and prayed, "Lord, thank You. All the obstacles I face in life will help me, not harm me. I will learn from them and somehow use these obstacles to give You glory. Thank You for this memorable day in my life."

Exhausted from his day's work, Johann went to his corner of the cooking room, laid down, and fell asleep.

A few days later, Johann went to town. When he approached the town square, he saw a beautiful young lady walking near the fountain. She sat on the fountain edge and displayed her book. Children from every direction flocked to her side. Tenderly, the young lady touched the faces of each child and spoke to every one of them. The children quietly sat down. After the young lady opened her book, she announced the book's title and began to read aloud.

Journey to the Glass Hill

Johann watched her intently and didn't pay attention to where the horses were walking. The team didn't want to hit the wall, so they abruptly stopped, causing Johann to tumble out of his seat. When the children saw it, they began to giggle. When the young lady turned her head toward the commotion, Johann turned red in the face. Quickly, he regained control of the team and guided the horses to the shopkeeper's store. The young woman watched Johann until he turned the corner with his wagon and disappeared from her view.

That was embarrassing, Johann thought as his face turned red again.

While Johann waited for the supplies, his curiosity got the better of him. So, he asked the shopkeeper, "Do you know anything about the group of children in the square listening to a story?"

"Ah. More likely you want to know who the lovely young lady is, right?" the shopkeeper replied with a smile.

D Marie

"Uh, yes," Johann answered back feeling his face warming up.

"The young lady is Princess Tea. The one I spoke of the last time you were here. Lovely, isn't she?"

"Yes, her parents must be very proud of her. She has a kind heart to take time to read to the children." Johann paused for a moment as he pictured the young woman sitting on the fountain ledge. Then, he noticed the shopkeeper staring at him. "It's getting late. I better finish up and get back to the farm. Goodbye, Sir."

"Goodbye, Johann," replied the shopkeeper, grinning knowingly.

As Johann drove the wagon back to the farm, he couldn't get the picture of the princess out of his head. "She looks familiar," he said to himself. "I pray she finds a man worthy of her."

Chapter 26

The Ride

The rising sun broke the darkness and revealed the black stallion standing by the rail fence. As he approached the corral, Johann noticed that the horse's bottom lip hung a little lower than normal, and his ears were slightly turned but loose. He didn't rear his head or stomp the ground. His demeanor reflected that of a saddle-broke horse.

"Why are you different today?" Johann asked. "Are you getting accustomed to me being around? I won't hurt you."

Johann sat on top of the fence. The stallion came over and stood right beside him. Gently, Johann rubbed the horse's neck. The horse turned his head toward Johann and looked him in the eyes. The stallion pointed his nose to his back and nodded to Johann.

"You want me to get on your back?" Johann asked the horse. At that moment, the horse exhaled through his nose and nudged the young man's leg. Johann remembered this docile response. Trusting his interpretation of horse body language, he stood up on the fence and stretched one of his legs over the bare back of this gorgeous horse. Slowly, he lowered his weight onto the stallion's back. The horse didn't budge an inch. Johann leaned forward, trusting the stallion with his whole body and hugged the horse's neck. Slowly, the stallion walked away from the fence.

"Amazing!" Johann exclaimed as he sat straight up with his hands in the air. "My first time on a horse, and it feels like I am king of the hill. Thank you, my friend. I will always be grateful to you."

D Marie

The horse picked up his pace and trotted faster. Johann leaned in closer since the stallion didn't have a halter or reins to help control him. The stallion was in control. The trot soon turned into a gallop. Johann held onto the horse's mane for dear life. The two become one as the stallion galloped through the pasture. Johann's hair, as well as the horse's mane and tail, fluttered in the wind. The stallion chose his path well. He galloped in a straight line until he reached the fence. Slowing down to a walk, he turned around and returned Johann back to

Journey to the Glass Hill

the barn. Johann loved the moment so much and didn't want to dismount. Reluctantly, he slid off the horse.

Standing in front of the muscular stallion, Johann pulled a carrot out of his pocket and fed him. The stallion carefully nibbled the carrot and nickered with approval. Slowly, the horse walked away. He paused for a moment, turned to look at Johann one more time, and galloped as fast as he could to the far corner of the pasture. His hoofs plowed into the soil, kicking dirt clods into the air as he made sharp twists and turns.

Wide-eyed, Johann shook his head in astonishment. "I'm glad you gave me an easy ride. I would have fallen off if you did that to me."

For the rest of the afternoon, Johann worked with the other horses. He tried to keep his attention focused on the horse training, but his mind kept straying to his ride on the stallion. As far as he knew, no one had ever ridden that horse before. That's why he never wore a halter.

When all the haltered horses had a turn on the course, Johann put his tools away. Exhausted by the day's events, he walked slumped shouldered toward the house. As he opened the cooking room door, he started thinking about his responsibilities for the next day.

"I better go to town tomorrow and replenish the supplies for the house. I want Father to be pleased with my work when he and my brothers return."

Early the next morning, Johann hitched up the team of horses to the wagon. He spotted the stallion on the far side of the pasture nibbling on the grass.

"Maybe I wore him out." Johann chuckled. "I'll bid him good morning as I pass by."

When Johann entered the town, he noticed a crowd standing in the square. He heard a banging noise that sounded like several hammers hitting wood at the same time. The peculiar noise came from the side wall of the palace. The royal stables and carriage house, which were connected to the palace wall, obscured that side of the palace from the town square. The horse pasture occupied the land behind these buildings, and it had a tall stone wall which also blocked the view.

Johann continued to guide his wagon toward the food shopkeeper's store. Once inside, he saw many unfamiliar people.

"Good morning, Johann!" the cheerful shopkeeper greeted him. "It's going to happen!"

"What's going to happen?" questioned Johann.

"Haven't you heard the news? The palace is building something."

"What are they making?"

"I don't know what, but something is being built."

"What is it being built for?" Johann probed further.

"I don't know that either, but something is different. Something is going to happen. I can feel it. Others can, too."

Many uncertainties but no answers, thought Johann. *I must come back in a few days to see if there is more information for my father.*

"Has anyone seen the carpenter lately?" yelled one of the customers, "I need his help."

"Not I," replied several others in the shop.

"I wonder where he is?" added the customer.

Chapter 27

Important Decision

A month prior to all the commotion around the mysterious building project, King Albert paced the floor. He stopped for a moment and asked, "What should I do?"

Queen Maria shared the same concern and walked over to his side. "Albert, this is a serious decision. The advice of many counselors may offer a solution."

"Excellent idea, Maria. Maybe one of them can guide us to the right choice."

King Albert called for his advisers and had them gather in the throne room. "Gentlemen," King Albert began, "Princess Tea, will soon be of age to marry. Tea has been educated by the best tutors in the land and has grown in knowledge and wisdom. When she marries, she and her husband will co-rule our kingdom of Christana someday."

"How can we be of help, King Albert?" the Head Counselor asked.

"I need your ideas for possible suitors for Tea," the king shared. "Ultimately, she will choose her intended."

The counselors thought about a selection process. They gave many suggestions: a ball for all the eligible bachelors, an archery contest, a horse race, or a jousting tournament. Other proposals were offered, too. One adviser even suggested he would be a suitable choice. The other counselors frowned and stared at the impetuous adviser showing their disapproval of that particular suggestion.

D Marie

"Thank you, gentlemen. You have given me many ideas. I need some time to ponder over them."

"You're welcome, King Albert," they replied. They reverently bowed to the king and exited the room.

With downcast eyes, Albert slowly returned to Maria.

"Maria, there were many good suggestions, but which one of them would produce a worthy choice for our daughter?" Albert lamented. "We need more help. Let's pray for guidance."

Holding hands and bowing their heads, Albert presented their petition to the Lord. "Dear Heavenly Father, we lift up Your Holy Name and praise You. We lay our need before You. We ask for Your wisdom and guidance. You know the perfect man who serves You now and will be a good husband for our daughter and a good king for Your people. Show us Your way, Father. We want to follow Your will. This we ask in Your Name. Amen."

With a tranquil voice, Maria asked, "Albert, what do *you want* in a son-by-marriage?"

King Albert's eyes opened wide. "Thank you, Maria. You gave me an idea!" he exclaimed. "Let's go see Tea."

Albert and Maria went to the garden to find Tea. They both stopped and quietly watched their daughter. Sitting on a bench by a shade tree, Tea was so involved with her book that she didn't notice her parents.

As Albert and Maria continued their walk, Maria spoke, "Tea, my dear one, your father and I have something to talk about with you. May we join you?"

Tea raised her head, smiled, and replied, "Of course. I was reading the book of Genesis when Abraham sent his servant to get his son, Isaac, a wife. The servant prayed and set up a plan for God to choose the right one."

Looking at Maria, Albert smiled. With a glow in his eyes, he tilted his head toward his daughter. "Tea, the time has come

Journey to the Glass Hill

for you to find your beloved. Will you trust God and your parents to find good choices for you to choose from?"

"Yes, Father!" replied Tea. "I trust you and our Heavenly Father."

"Thank you, Tea. There will be a contest," her father shared. "We will get started on it right away."

The royal artisans were called to make a wooden hill. They employed Hans, the local carpenter, for his expertise. Sworn to secrecy, all the workers remained inside the palace walls until they finished the project. Disguising the noise proved to be impossible. The townsfolk could hear it but could only speculate its purpose.

Princess Tea continued to read to the children in the town square, but the palace guards stood watch by her. Only children could come near her to listen to the story.

One day, the wooden structure emerged over the palace wall and became visible from the town square. The townsfolk asked even more questions, but the palace offered no response. At this point, Princess Tea remained in the palace and discontinued her story readings in the square.

Billowing smoke rose above the palace grounds adding to the confusion and mystery. Soon, something that reflected the sun's light became visible from the top of the wooden mound. As time passed, this substance covered more areas of the wooden structure.

"What is the king creating?" the local people constantly asked. They wanted to question the guards, but if someone did try to approach the palace entrance, the guards quickly crossed their long lances. No one dared to proceed any further and slowly backed away.

One day, the noise stopped, the smoke disappeared, and the palace doors opened. Guards dressed in their finest tunics and royal tabards came out of the palace with individual parchments to be placed on the announcement boards throughout the kingdom. Hans, the carpenter, followed the guards. He had a knowing smile on his face, but he had to wait until the posting of the parchment before he could proceed. Eagerly, everyone ran to the board to read the announcement:

*King Albert and Queen Maria
invite all eligible young men to compete in a contest
for the hand in marriage of
Princess Dorothea.
The Princess will sit on top of the hill made of glass.
All eligible suitors must ride up the hill on a horse.
The winner will receive a golden apple.
Three golden apples will be awarded to
three separate contestants.
Princess Dorothea will make her choice from
the winning contestants.
Any rider, failing to climb the hill on his horse,
will be disqualified.
The contest will begin on September 30.
May the Lord be with you.*

The mystery was revealed, a chance to marry the princess in one month's time. News of the contest spread quickly. Suitors of all shapes and sizes journeyed to Christana. The town bustled with excitement.

The news reached the village where Ari and his sons stayed. A traveler, who stopped at the inn, shared the announcement he had recently read. Magnus and Ivar stared at each other before looking at their father. It did not take long for them to pack up and head for home.

"We have sold all of our best horses. The ones at home are not saddle trained yet," Ari commented. "We have work to do."

"Papa," Magnus pointed out, "our personal horses are the best. Ivar and I will each win one of the golden apples. Do we want anyone to win the third apple?"

Journey to the Glass Hill

"Magnus," marveled Ari, "you are right. One of my sons will be king!"

"And it's going to be me," quipped Magnus. "I'll let you two visit as often as you like."

This response left Ivar feeling indignant, and he glared at his brother.

"Sons!" Ari interjected. "Neither of you will win if we do not work together. Now let's get going. I am eager to start practicing."

A few days after the posted announcement, Johann went to town. He knew his family would be coming back soon as they had never been gone this long before. When he drove closer to the town square, he couldn't believe his eyes. People of all ages filled the square. Some of the men raised their voices to each other. Some bowed to each other as if they were royalty then laughed about it.

Johann kept going. He didn't want to get involved with their merrymaking. Stopping in front of the food shopkeeper, he saw the carpenter outside making new signs. Entering the shop, Johann paused while some patrons argued with the shopkeeper.

"This cost less last week," one shopper said raising his voice. "Why is it more today?"

"Because the visitors for the contest will pay more," the shopkeeper replied in a sarcastic tone. "Do you want it or not?"

As the shopkeeper lifted his head, he spotted Johann. "Johann, my boy. Good to see you. I told you it was coming!"

"What is coming?" Johann inquired.

"Are you the only one in Christana who doesn't know?"

"Know what?"

"The contest for the princess's hand in marriage!" the shopkeeper yelled with excitement. "It could be you. You are eligible. Do you have a horse to ride? You must ride a horse up the hill of glass. Didn't you see it when you came to the square? The announcement is on the public board."

D Marie

Johann had been so busy staring at the people in the square that he hadn't noticed the new shining hill behind the palace stables. Curiosity ate away at him, but he remained calm and finished his business in the shop first. He loaded the wagon and made his way to the front of the palace. As Johann turned into the square, he saw the top of the hill gleaming in the sunlight.

After he dismounted the wagon, Johann quickly walked to the announcement board. Johann's mouth dropped open as he read the news. Princess Tea will choose one of the three winners to be her beloved.

"I pray for the man who wins. May he be worthy of Tea," Johann said in a muffled voice. "Father will want to know about this as soon as he returns home."

Gently, Johann guided the team of horses away from the square and toward the lane where he lived. As he rounded the corner in the lane, he saw three horses tied up by the barn.

They're back! Johann thought. *I must tell them the news immediately.*

After he secured the team, Johann ran into the house carrying the supplies. He found Ari, Magnus, and Ivar laughing and having a good time.

"It's about time you showed up!" Ari yelled at Johann. "Where have you been?"

"Sir," said Johann ignoring the question, "I have great news from town."

"Hmm," Ari teased, "could it be about a contest to marry the princess and be king?"

"Yes. How did you know?"

"The news is spreading far away from here. We have ridden a great distance, and we're hungry. Fix us some food."

"Yes, Sir!"

"And you can call me Sire when I win the contest," Magnus taunted. "I will let you live in the palace, too, in the cooking room." Ari and the twins laughed.

Journey to the Glass Hill

Tomorrow is another day, Johann thought. The memory of Grandma Elina came to his mind, and he remembered her words, "The Lord provides, Johann." A smile spread across his face.

Ari noticed. *What's he up to? I better watch him closely.*

Chapter 28

The Contest

One by one, eligible bachelors from far away villages and towns journeyed to Christana. The competitors glared at their competition as they searched for the local inns. Some of the suitors preferred to keep guard over their horses and stayed with them in the stables.

The out-of-town suitors had unusual competitors. Finely dressed men and women, arriving in elegant carriages, wanted to attend the festive occasion. Both groups converged at the local inns demanding a place to stay. Neighboring villagers came to see the exciting contest, too.

The innkeeper, closest to the palace, did not concern himself with the contest. He looked around inside his inn, seeing paying customers in every room. His wife took over the cooking while he served his guests. Concern appeared on his face as he inspected his coin drawer. *I have never had this many coins in here. I need to hide them somewhere.*

The merchants selling in the market enjoyed their good fortune. Fresh fruits and vegetables, piled high on tables, enticed the hungry shoppers. Kettles hanging over small fires kept the simmering stews warm and ready to eat. Some vendors even sold devices to help the horses climb the hill.

No one knew what would work since practicing on the hill of glass was not permitted. Straddling the palace wall, the glass hill flowed into the pasture where the palace horses roamed. The exterior stone wall of the pasture became taller by adding a solid wooden fence on top of it to hide the construction of the hill. After the announcement of the contest, the temporary

D Marie

wooden fence came down revealing a grander view of this magnificent hill. Posted sentries on the exterior ramparts guarded the glass hill all day and all night. Access to the hill would be through a side entrance in the pasture wall.

The amazing hill glistened in the sunlight. During the night, it reflected the torch light of the sentries. The fire seemed to dance on the hill's surface. Hues of yellow, orange, and red blanketed the slippery slope. The larger view elevated the tension in the air.

All the single men wanted to win one of the golden apples. Many boasted that their horse would succeed and reach the top of the hill. Arrogance and pride abounded everywhere.

Ari stared at his sons as they worked with the horses. He contemplated the significance of winning this contest and decided to keep his oldest sons and their horses at the farm. Only Johann traveled to town for supplies.

Magnus and Ivar devoted their time to prepare for the contest. They constructed a hill of dirt and covered it with wooden planks tightly fastened together. Magnus and Ivar tried different approaches to the artificial hill to get their horses accustomed to the climb.

Ivar climbed to the top on his first attempt. After his descent, he turned his head toward Magnus and gave his brother a smug grin. Magnus burned inside with indignation. He dug his heels into his horse's side. His horse galloped straight for the hill and abruptly stopped at the base. Magnus almost fell off.

Ivar guided his horse toward his brother and patted him on the back. "Try again." Magnus did and went to the top of the hill. Ivar nodded in approval.

Magnus and Ivar often ignored their duties with the haltered horses and passed the responsibility to their younger brother. When Johann walked out toward the barn, Ari noticed the black stallion coming to greet him. Although Johann didn't work with the stallion, he talked to him and rubbed his neck and head. Afterward, he gave the stallion a carrot. The interaction concerned Ari.

This is the only horse, besides the twin's horses, that could charge up the glass hill, Ari contemplated. *I better make sure he is not capable of going anywhere near that hill.*

Johann shortened the workout time with each horse. His mind focused on his next duty: to prepare the evening meal. After he departed for the house, he looked back and noticed his father going into the barn near the area where the stallion stood.

All evening long, Magnus and Ivar boasted about their expertise of horsemanship. Johann had to endure their never-ending, patronizing talk and their regular rudeness. After the meal, Johann remained in the cooking room while the others sat in the adjoining room.

Johann glanced at the pile of rags where he hid his mother's Bible. He missed reading the Scriptures. They fed his soul and spirit. "Perhaps, I will have a place of my own where I can read my Bible anytime I want. Someday I will, for I know the Lord provides," he whispered.

The following day, when Johann went to the barn to begin working with the horses, he noticed the stallion had a slight limp.

"Did you hurt your ankle?" Johann asked the stallion. He leaned over to get a closer look at the horse's leg and detected no visible injury. "No running for you today. Take it easy until your leg is better." Then, he offered a carrot in his opened hand, and the horse ate it.

The stallion lifted his head and shook it. Afterward, he slowly walked away as if he understood what Johann had just said.

Chapter 29

Brass

Royal banners, mounted on the street corners, fluttered in the breeze while the visitors and out of town suitors admired their vibrant colors. The enticement of the contest brought many strangers to Christana. It also brought beggars to town. Beggars were rarely seen before. Most of the unfortunate people were given assistance to find a place to live and work. The townsfolk took care of their own people.

Some of the beggars were in real need while others just wanted to make some easy money. One old man, in tattered clothes, went from house to house asking for food. In return, he offered to do some work for the owner. He heard many excuses but received very little food. Turning his attention to the local inns, he approached the contestants, offering his services to care for their horses or do errands for them. Ignoring him was the kindest response. Most of the suitors scolded or teased the old man.

As the first day of the contest approached, the tension in the air increased. The competing suitors placed their faith in posturing with each other. Some puffed their chests out displaying their pride. Others lifted their chins, refusing to make eye contact. Another group used the I'll-win-and-you-won't look, trying to stare down their competition. They all had their eyes focused on the glass hill.

After confining the palace's horses in the stables, the guards thoroughly cleansed the grassy pasture surrounding the glass hill. Following the orders of the king, the sentries pushed open the heavy wooden side doors to the pasture displaying the

D Marie

full view of the glass hill for the first time. Curious spectators and eager suitors gathered at the doorway. The glass glistened in the sunlight causing them to squint and shield their eyes. Its brilliance made it impossible to climb during the daytime, therefore, the contest would be held in a few hours when the sun set. Everyone went to their places of rest for the evening meal.

To give each rider a guaranteed turn on the hill, King Albert amended the terms of the contest. All successful climbers of the glass hill would receive a golden apple. Previously, everyone wanted to be first since there were only three apples. Now, any rider who went first and failed offered some insight for the following contestants in their approach to climb the glass hill.

The beggars began their rounds early since no one would be home during the contest that night. One of the beggars came to the house of Ari and knocked on the door. Being curious, Magnus answered the door and found the beggar standing in the entranceway. Before he could offer to work for food, Magnus laughed in the man's face and shut the door. Taking a deep breath, the old man turned and walked away shuffling his feet. Johann heard Magnus making fun of the old man. He had compassion for the beggar and quickly picked up some food. Quietly tiptoeing, he went out the back door and approached the old man.

"Sir," Johann said, "here is some food. Please stay the night in our barn. I will bring you a blanket later."

The old man smiled and gratefully accepted the food and lodging. "You are a kind young man. May the Lord bless you."

"Thank you," Johann replied and returned to the cooking room.

As sunset approached, Princess Tea paused at the doorway and breathed deeply. She agreed with her parents about the contest, but the unpredictability of the winner still bothered her. A

Journey to the Glass Hill

familiar phrase came to her memory, "The Lord provides." Immediately, Tea lowered her head and prayed, "Heavenly Father, I trust You as I trust my earthly father. I know You have the perfect choice for my future beloved. I submit to Your will. In Jesus' Name, I pray. Amen." Afterward, Tea raised her head and proceeded through the courtyard to reach the top of the hill made of glass.

Sturdy wooden stairs began in the courtyard and ascended to the top of the palace wall. The glass hill cascaded from the top of the wall onto the pasture grass on the other side. An elegant chair with golden apples waited for the princess. Getting up the hill from the pasture side presented a puzzling challenge. The slippery surface would be difficult to climb with a horse.

One by one, the mounted suitors gathered at the base of the glass hill. The anxious contestants arrived early before the sun had set. Dressed in various forms of attire, they waited for their turn to climb the hill. Spectators stood near the side giving the riders a wide berth to avoid being stepped on by the horses.

Magnus and Ivar finished their preparations for the contest. With an attitude of self-confidence, the two brothers and their father rode away on the only saddle-broke horses. Johann remained at home with nothing to ride.

One by one, the suitors directed their horses toward the hill. The spectators cheered the riders as their horses placed their front hoofs on the hill. Unfortunately, the horses could not get traction on the slick surface of the glass. Dejected, the riders and their horses lowered their heads and backed away from the base of the hill.

After his father and brothers left for the contest, Johann hastened to check on the beggar. Carrying a blanket and more food, he gently pushed the barn door open and called for the old man. "Hello, I'm here." No one answered, but he did hear a strange noise coming from the back of the barn. Johann's hand slightly trembled as he grabbed the handle, pulled, and

D Marie

opened the back door. There staring him in the eyes stood a large brown steed that snorted and pawed the ground. The horse was fully tacked with the finest saddle and bridle trimmed in brilliant brass. Next to the horse, exquisite riding clothes and boots laid on a wooden box. A helmet trimmed in shining brass completed the outfit.

Johann cautiously looked at the horse. Their eyes met. The horse looked at Johann and then looked at the clothes resting on a box. The young man tried on the clothes and helmet. The clothes fit perfectly. Johann had never worn boots before, only his brothers and father had them. He marveled at the feel of the leather hugging his legs. The snug helmet required a little effort to pull over his head, but it would not fall off. Chainmail hung from the rear and sides of the headpiece. This covered his hair and the sides of his face. No one would recognize Johann in this outfit.

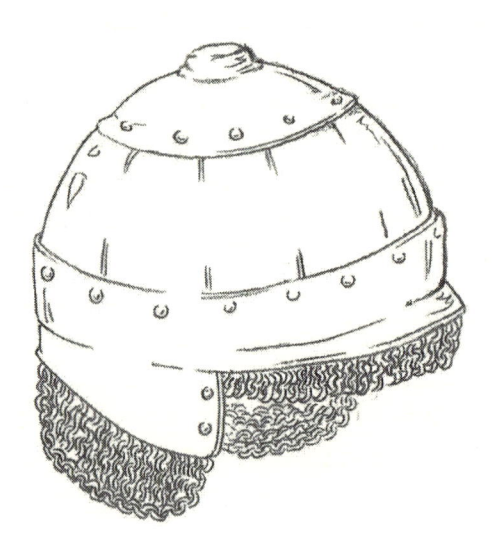

The stallion turned his head and pointed his nose to the saddle. Johann climbed on the box where the clothes had been and bravely mounted the horse. Immediately, the horse bolted from the post and headed for town.

Journey to the Glass Hill

Initially, fear started to bother Johann. *This isn't my horse. What would happen if I get caught?*

The words, "The Lord provides," began to rise in Johann, and he put his trust in those words. Peace came and filled his whole body as the horse galloped down the lane and went straight toward the crowd. All too soon, they stood in front of the glass hill. Princess Tea had started to gather the golden apples resting in her lap so she could stand up, but when she saw another rider approaching, she waved for him to try.

Johann talked to his mount and guided him to the foot of the glass hill. The steed snorted. The vapor of his breath rose from his nostrils on this chilly evening like smoke from a fire. He let out a loud neigh. Tea raised her arms up in the air to encourage the rider to conquer the hill. The horse reared up on his hind legs. Johann leaned toward the horse's neck, clinched his legs tight, and grasped the pommel of the saddle just in time. The stallion jumped forward and raced toward the top of the hill.

The horse and rider climbed one-third of the way up before the horse lost his momentum. His quivering leg muscles strained to continue the climb, but the horse slid backward.

Tea had never seen any of the other riders get their whole horse on the hill. She stood up and tossed the rider one of the golden apples. "Here is your reward." Johann caught it and rode away before anyone could get near him.

Johann quickly guided the steed back to the farm. Fortunately, his father and brothers had stayed in town with the other riders, likely trying to figure out the identity of the unknown rider. Johann immediately changed his clothes and fed the horse.

He paused to admire his prize. The apple glistened in the faint moonlight as he held it in his hand. Johann's mind raced with thought, *What shall I do now?* Looking around, he decided to hide the golden apple in the barn. After gathering the blanket and food, he returned to the house.

D Marie

Before first light, Johann quietly tiptoed out of the house and ran to the barn. He saw three horses tied to the rail, but those were the horses his father and brothers rode. When he looked behind the barn, the horse he had ridden the night before had been taken away. The clothes, helmet, and box had disappeared, too.

The town buzzed with exhilaration about the mystery rider. If this rider could master the hill, then who else would be able to climb it?

Concern dominated the thoughts of the royal family, because this mystery rider might be the future king someday. Princess Tea tried to imagine what the rider might look like without his helmet. The royal couple wanted to know if he would be a good husband for their daughter and a good king for their people.

The next morning, the twins sat in the cooking room waiting for their morning meal. Magnus slammed his fist on the table. "I want to know who this rider is and where he came from."

Ivar slumped over the table and rested his head in his hands. "No one recognized the horse, the set of clothes, or the helmet. He must be from a distant town or country."

"Nobody else could climb the hill," Ari said hanging his head down and staring at the empty food bowl in front of him. "I guess the contest is over."

The palace issued a royal decree. Whoever had the golden apple should come forward and meet the royal family. Later that afternoon, King Albert, Queen Maria, and Princess Tea, dressed in their finest garments, waited for the champion to redeem his golden apple. No one came.

The feeling of dread gripped Johann. "How can I explain what I have done using someone else's horse and clothes? I can't go. I'll get in trouble."

Journey to the Glass Hill

When no one came forward, King Albert declared that the contest would continue. Everyone in the kingdom cheered, and the eligible men concentrated on their next tactics.

Chapter 30

Silver

The vendors put their hill climbing devices back on display and waited for the suitors. They watched with amusement as the eager competitors rummaged through the clamps looking for the right size for their horses. Everyone was happy until payment time.

"This is more than yesterday's price," one irritated suitor said.

"When you're king, you will have all the coins you need," replied the shrewd vendor. The man grudgingly finished his purchase.

One of the beggar-men overheard the suitor and vendor. *No prospects here*, he thought, and he passed them by. He knocked on many doors and went into many shops. The old man always offered to work for the food, but disappointment followed him, resulting in little or nothing to eat. The other beggars fared the same. Some of the townsfolk focused only on themselves and forgot about the charity for others.

When the old man came to Ari's farm he lifted his weary arm and knocked on the front door. Ivar opened the door and glared at the visitor. Noticing he wasn't someone of importance, Ivar talked sternly to the old man and chased him away.

D Marie

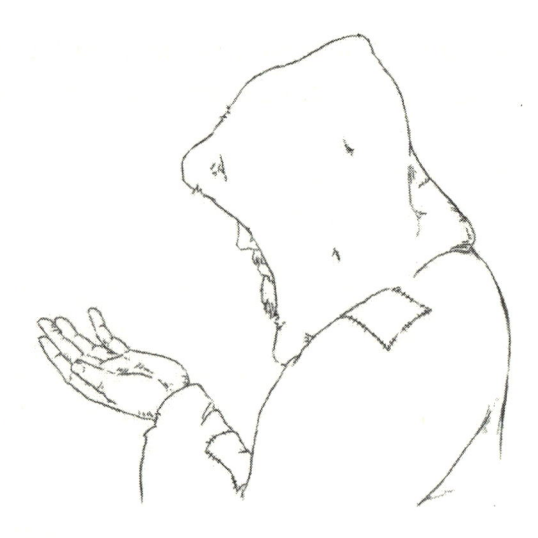

Johann witnessed the harsh treatment, and his heart went out to the old man again. He left the house and found him walking in the lane with his head hanging down. Johann's kind and caring voice touched the beggar's heart, and he followed the young man back to the barn.

Johann quietly gathered food, water, and his warm blanket from the cooking room and returned to the barn. "Thank you," the old man said. "I will enjoy this food, and the blanket is appreciated as the nights are getting colder."

Magnus and Ivar yelled for Johann. "They need me to help them get ready for the contest," Johann said grimly.

The old man smiled, winked at him, and told him, "Go, young man. I'll be all right."

"Goodbye, Sir. I'll come back later."

Hurrying as fast as he could, Johann helped Magnus and Ivar so he could return to the barn. They strutted in front of the metal mirror with their finest clothes on, and their appearance pleased their father. Magnus and Ivar ordered Johann to get their horses. He untied them from the rail and walked them to the front of the house. Johann handed over the reins, and the horse sellers rode to town.

Journey to the Glass Hill

Indignation tempted Johann's feelings as he watched his father and brothers disappear down the lane. *It would be easy to give in to anger,* he thought. *But I'm not doing that. I'll stand on the Word of God.* Johann resisted, and the negative feelings fled. His faith produced victory and peace.

Johann focused his attention on the beggar and ran to the barn. Surveying the interior, he noted that the blanket, food, and the old man were gone. "I hope he stays warm tonight."

As the young man picked up the dishes, a loud thud thundered from the barn wall. Johann shuddered. He set the food tray down and cautiously opened the back door. A stunning horse as black as night pawed the ground and flared his nostrils. Steam like vapor, coming from his mouth, filled the chilled air. Shining silver adorned the horse's saddle and reins. Next to the horse, Johann saw riding garments and a silver helmet that glimmered in the setting sun.

The horse nodded at Johann and nickered. The low, vibrating sound put the young man at ease. "I don't need encouragement this time to put on the riding attire." After he dressed into the new clothes, Johann mounted the horse, and the steed raced to town.

Princess Tea patiently waited for a successful champion. Her fingers clutched the golden apples on her lap. She watched the suitors maneuver their horses toward the hill. The horses pawed at the hill trying to climb it. The rough surface of the hoof devices dug into the smooth glass, but the horses were not able to get all four of their hoofs on the hill at the same time.

When the princess saw a new rider approaching the base of the hill, she smiled and raised her arms. Without hesitation, Johann's horse reared up on his hind legs, gave a big jump, and started to climb the hill. But, at the halfway mark, the stallion lost his strength and slid backward. The princess stood up and tossed an apple to the rider just in time. "Your reward, my champion." Johann caught it and nodded to the princess.

D Marie

Once they were back on the ground, Johann guided his horse through the gate, and they disappeared into the night.

The horse returned the amazed rider to the barn. Johann dismounted. His hands slid across the muscular neck of the magnificent steed. His eyes looked around to see if anyone was near and quickly changed back into his own clothes. He fed the black stallion and curried him with tender care. Johann placed the second golden apple near the first one and declared, "I'm going to stay and find out who is bringing and retrieving these horses." After an hour of waiting, Johann's enthusiasm subsided, and his eyelids became heavy. He tried to keep them open, but he soon fell fast asleep. Johann woke up and found himself alone, shivering in the chilly, damp morning air.

At daybreak, Magnus walked into the cooking room and stamped his foot on the floor. "Who is this mystery rider? I have never seen a horse breed like those two stallions that went up the hill. What makes them different? Did you see them jump?"

"Where is Johann?" asked Ivar. "Why hasn't he fixed our morning meal?"

The townsfolk and visitors gathered in the square staring at the palace entrance. Everyone looked for the two finely dressed winners to ride in on their horses holding their golden apples. "They should be arriving soon," a hopeful spectator said.

The palace displayed a somber tone. The princess sighed, "At least I'll have two champions to choose from. Why are they waiting to come forward?"

King Albert paced the floor then sat down. His right hand supported his chin while his elbow rested on the arm of his throne. Queen Maria wrung her hands as she quietly sat next to Albert. They hoped the winning suitor would be the right choice to be their daughter's husband and the future king.

Journey to the Glass Hill

Again, the decree went out for the recipients of the golden apples to appear. The royal family prepared themselves for the champion, but no one showed up.

Johann knew about the decree. He heard his father talk about it. "I want to meet Princess Tea, but I fear I'll get in trouble for using someone else's horse," he whispered in the solitude of the cooking room, and he stayed home. The next day, the contest continued. The anxious princess would have to wait for a successful suitor.

Chapter 31

Gold

The tension in Christana escalated. Many residents and visitors fed their empty concept of self-importance by being rude to each other and to those of little importance. Unkind words fell on the beggars' ears. Helping hands became instruments to push the disadvantaged away. Even the innkeeper, who used to give them the leftover food, shunned the beggar-men and told them to move on.

Magnus and Ivar did the same thing when they saw a beggar-man coming down the lane in the early afternoon. They both hurled insults at him. The two brothers, pleased with their callousness to the beggar, went back into the house.

Johann saw it and ran down the lane to find him. "Please Sir, come to the barn. I assure you; I will take care of you." The old man, touched by the young man's kindness, stroked his beard and followed Johann.

"Why do you bother with me?" the old man asked.

"It's what I enjoy doing, taking care of God's people. My grandmother taught me that the Lord provides. Sometimes, His provision uses human hands and hearts. I'll come back and check on you later."

"Thank you," the beggar replied with a warm smile.

When Johann returned to the cooking room, Magnus and Ivar were there and ordered him to get them ready.

"I feel lucky today," Magnus boasted. "I'm wearing a helmet tonight like the mystery riders. This has to be the trick to get up the glass hill."

"I'm going to win an apple tonight! You just watch me!" shouted Ivar. "I'm winning tonight, and I'm not sharing my secret weapon with anyone, least of all you."

With those words, anger rose up in Magnus. His eyes narrowed as he charged after Ivar.

Quickly, Ari stepped between the two brothers and shouted. "Sons! If we don't get to town, the contest will be over and neither of you will win."

Johann had to prepare Magnus' helmet. Polishing the helmet reminded him of the ones he had worn. *I don't think this will help you, Magnus*, he thought with a grin. Every time Johann got close to the back door to leave, Magnus and Ivar demanded more assistance. Hours went by before Johann could get to the barn. Finally, the twins were ready and rode away with their father.

After he gathered some food and drink, Johann went to serve the old man. The barn door refused to open. He leaned his shoulder into it, but the stubborn door would not budge. "Open the door. It's me, Johann," he called out, but no one responded.

Johann dropped the dishes and ran to the back door of the barn. There, staring him in the face, stood the most magnificent white horse he had ever seen. His long mane and tail flowed in the air as the mighty steed shook his head and body. Although his hair was white, his skin appeared to be black. The saddle and bridle were trimmed in glistening gold. Clothes made of the finest cloth, boots made of the best leather, and a helmet trimmed in gold were neatly laid out on the box near the white stallion.

Being more concerned for the beggar, Johann entered the back door and checked the inside of the barn. The old man had left. "Maybe, he was tired of waiting. I wonder if the beggar saw who brought the horse? Next time, I'll ask."

Johann turned his attention back to the white horse. Without delay, he put on the clothes, boots, and helmet. He

Journey to the Glass Hill

mounted the steed, took the reins of the horse, and confidently steered him toward the glass hill. Johann noticed an open path in the pasture, and he charged the hill. The muscular horse reared up on his hind legs and leaped forward onto the slippery slope. Successfully maneuvering the glass hill, he went all the way to the top.

Princess Tea stood up and walked toward Johann. Up close, he saw her kind eyes and lovely face. Her graceful movements revealed her poise and confidence. He reminisced about seeing her at a distance, sitting by the fountain reading to the children.

Tea handed him a golden apple. None of the other riders could master the glass hill. "My champion," she said as the other riders tried to crawl up the hill.

Johann didn't want to reveal himself on the borrowed horse and quickly spoke, "I will return!"

Tea watched the newest champion ride down the hill and gallop through the gate. *The contest is over. When will the three champions present themselves?* She wondered. *How will I decide which champion to choose?*

When Ari returned home, he found the broken dishes by the barn and yelled, "Johann, what were you doing with dishes all the way out here? Why are you so careless?" Truthfully, he was upset that his twin sons had not won a golden apple. A month of anticipation turned into a mountain of disappointment. If he only knew about his son, Johann, and his victory.

Chapter 32

The Reunion

Johann tossed and turned all night. His eyes sprang open each time he tried to keep them shut. He could not wait any longer. At daybreak, he put on his best clothes. Johann looked around the cooking room one more time. So many emotions ran through his mind. He closed his eyes and prayed for his father and brothers.

It was time to leave. Johann opened the back door and walked to the barn. Although he knew he wouldn't find anything, he opened the back door of the barn. *The horse and clothing have vanished. Why am I not surprised?* he mused to himself as he retrieved the three golden apples.

As he walked to town, thoughts of how to approach the palace flooded his mind. "What do I do when I get there? Lord, help me." When he approached the entrance, the guards crossed their lances and refused to let him in.

"What business do you have with the king?" one of the guards snarled at him. "Can't you see he doesn't have time for you?"

I can't tell them what I have, Johann thought. *What am I going to do? Jesus help me.*

The commotion reached the windows of the throne room. King Albert walked onto the balcony and asked, "What is going on?"

"A laborer wants to see you. I told him to go away," replied the head guard.

"Send him in," the king demanded.

D Marie

"Yes, Sire," the guard humbly replied as he lowered his head.

The anticipation made Johann so nervous that he didn't think his legs would carry him. They were somewhat unsteady and wobbly as he walked. The palms of his hands perspired and became clammy. An odd pain in his gut intensified. Johann said a quiet prayer to himself, *Lord give me strength*, and the Lord provided.

The guards guided him into the room where the royal family waited. When he stopped at the appropriate distance, Johann bowed before King Albert, Queen Maria, and Princess Tea who sat on thrones. He raised his head and looked at King Albert in the eyes. Immediately, Johann fell to his knees.

The king smiled, winked at him, and asked, "You have something for me?"

With trembling hands, Johann pulled the three golden apples from his pouch and gave them to—the beggar? Johann's eyes widened in shock as he saw the resemblance between the king and the beggar. This time, the beggar was clean shaven, neatly groomed, dressed in royal clothes, and sat on a throne.

King Albert had devised a challenge that only specially trained horses would be able to climb. The horses were given only to those who proved themselves to be compassionate to the people he would rule over someday. Johann was the only

Journey to the Glass Hill

one who consistently demonstrated the qualities of a good king by caring for his people.

Albert stood up, walked over to the bewildered young man, and sat down next to him at the edge of the dais.

"Johann," Albert began, "the first time I saw your parents was in church. I had just returned to Christana with my betrothed, Maria. They came in as I was praying with Reverend Gudmund to ask the Lord for His blessings and guidance. Your parents were there to arrange for their marriage. After your birth, I was there at your baptism. In fact, I asked to be your godfather. When you were almost three, your mother passed away. You and your grandmother lived here at the palace for a year. Maria taught you how to read. For two more years, you and your grandmother came to the palace every day to care for Tea. You and Tea grew up together for those three years. Before your grandmother passed away, she made arrangements for Reverend Gudmund to live in her home. He played hymns for you to hear. Tea was there every week receiving music lessons. After Gudmund's death, the cottage was willed to me. It is now yours. When I saw Rex get excited as you entered the square, I knew it was you. You were now allowed to come to town. I arranged for you to deliver manure to the palace garden to see if you could still read and calculate numbers. Tea was permitted to read in the square so you could see her and for Tea to see you. I came to your house, a few years ago, to be with you."

"That was you in the old clothes? You have been looking after me all these years? Grandma was right. The Lord provides." He pulled his necklace and locket out from under his shirt and opened it.

Tea intently watched. She reached for her necklace with a similar locket as Johann's and opened it. The locket had an identical cross on one side and the words "I love you" on the other side.

D Marie

"Tea," her father shared, "your locket was given to your mother and me as a wedding present from Johann's mother."

At this point, tears streamed down Johann's face. Tea noticed. She walked toward him and sat on the dais by Johann and her father.

"You were my first playmate and friend as a child. You are the one who fell off the wagon seat as you watched me in the square," Tea reminisced. "You have shown kindness to all who come near you. You trust and serve the Lord. You came up the glass hill and stole my heart. Johann, you are the one I choose as my champion and my beloved."

Maria stood up and walked over to Johann, hugged him, and said, "Welcome home, Son. We have missed you dearly."

Lowering his head, Johann offered a prayer. "Thank You Lord for providing. I love You, Jesus."

From that moment, Johann never had to live on the farm down the lane. He never had to sleep in the cooking room again. He embraced his new family, but at the same time, he felt a void in his heart for his father and brothers.

Chapter 33

The Revelation

The revelation of Johann's victory traveled quickly. The bells in Christana rang for a long period of time. Immediately, sentries mounted their horses and traveled in every direction announcing the good news. "Johann, son of Ari, is the winner of the Glass Hill contest."

They even rode by Ari's farm. When Magnus and Ivar heard the news, they went into a fit of rage.

"How could he do this to us?" Magnus ranted. "He kept secrets from us."

"What else did he keep secret?" Ivar added.

Since the only room in the house where Johann spent most of his time was the cooking room, Magnus and Ivar went inside and searched every shelf and corner. They looked under the stack of wood for the fireplace. They turned over his bedding in the corner. They found nothing but a set of old clothes they used to wear.

The revelation of Johann being the future king of Christana stunned Ari. He remained outside, looked upward at the sky, then closed his eyes. The warmth of the sun felt good on his face. Ari lowered his head and walked over to where his beloved was buried. He sat there for hours.

He watched the flowers sway back and forth in the morning breeze. The grass offered a sweet fragrance, but he received no comfort.

Ari's wish had come true. Johann was out of his house. However, Ari felt depleted. He had achieved no victory, no joy.

D Marie

Being hungry, Magnus and Ivar called out, "Johann, where's our…" Then, the realization of their situation sank in. They had to do all the housework, including fixing the food, which was a challenge since everything was put away.

"What do you do first?" Ivar asked Magnus.

"I have no idea," Magnus replied. "The fire needs wood. Get some."

Ivar threw a log on the embers in the fireplace. Ashes flew through the air.

"Look at the mess you made, Ivar!" hollered Magnus. "Go get something to clean it up."

Ivar's eyes scanned the room and landed on a pile of rags. He went over and grabbed some. When he did, he noticed something next to the remaining rags in the pile. He leaned over and picked up a book. As Ivar looked closer, he saw the words, *Holy Bible*, on the cover.

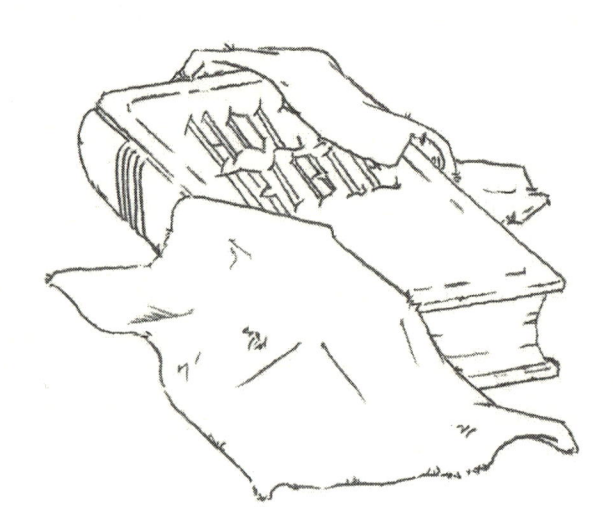

"Magnus!" Ivar shouted.

"Now, what?" Magnus snapped back.

"I found something. Look at this!" Ivar exclaimed.

Journey to the Glass Hill

Carefully, they opened the Book. It fell open to the Book of Johann.

"What does it say, Ivar?"

"Some man named Jesus says He is the Bread of Life, and you will not go hungry if you come to Him. If you believe in Him, you will not be thirsty."

Both brothers sat down and read more. Indeed, they were not hungry for food at that moment. They were hungry for the Word of God. The more they read, the more their hearts were convicted. They read for several hours.

While Ari sat near the area where his Johanna was buried, he fell asleep. When he woke up, his neck ached, and he rubbed it. Realizing he had not eaten for a while, he slowly walked to the house. He found Magnus and Ivar praying at the table. Tears streamed down their faces. When they looked up, they saw their father as he stared at them.

"Father," Magnus said, "we have been so wrong. We have treated Johann shamefully. Ivar and I want to correct that wrong."

No! screamed through Ari's mind.

Summoning his strength, his voice stammered and cracked, "What are you planning to do?"

"We are going to see Johann, if he will see us, and humbly submit our apologies," Ivar replied.

Ari silently assessed the situation. *I'm losing control. What can I do?* He took a deep breath and released it. His demeanor changed. The eyebrows that were once relaxed now pulled together. The muscles on his jaw tightened as he clenched his teeth. With a stern voice and glaring eyes, he said, "If you do that, don't come back!"

Magnus and Ivar knew that look. Previously, they had buckled under his pressure and gave in. This time, the Word resided in them.

Ivar looked at Magnus. "I'll understand if you want to stay."

D Marie

"I can't," Magnus replied.

Ari tried another tactic. "Don't you realize what you are giving up? Your home, your income, your inheritance." In a softer voice, he added, "me."

The twins had only one choice. Their hearts could not be healed if they did not go to Johann. They gathered up their belongings and bid their father farewell.

They plodded their way to town. Since they hadn't eaten all day, Magnus and Ivar stopped at the inn for a meal. The innkeeper looked surprised to see them so early in the day. When he came to their table, the innkeeper saw the sorrowful looks on their faces. He took their order and returned to his other customers. Reverend Lars also noticed their dejected faces. He carried his plate to Magnus' and Ivar's table.

"May I join you?" he asked politely and sat down.

Magnus and Ivar looked up to see the man sitting down. Even though they didn't know him, they could tell he was a man of the church.

"Uh," Magnus finally spoke, "how do we address you?"

"Lars," he replied in a cheerful voice, "my name is Lars."

"Lars," Magnus continued, "we have done so many wrong things, and now we are full of sorrow for our sins."

"Perhaps I can help," Lars offered in an encouraging tone. "If you want to share, I am here to listen."

Magnus and Ivar talked for a long time. They weren't even hungry enough to finish their food. When they completed pouring out their hearts to Reverend Lars, they asked, "What can we do to be forgiven?"

"Forgiveness is a gift from the one you have offended," Lars offered. "Speak with Johann. He has a good heart and a generous spirit. Spiritual forgiveness comes when you repent and are right with the Lord."

"We knew very little about the Lord until we read a Bible this morning," Ivar interjected. "How can we learn more on a deeper level? There were many parts that were difficult to understand."

"How much do you want to learn?" inquired Lars.

"Everything!" both said together.

"There is a place of learning, a university, for men who want to be ministers and do the Lord's work," Lars continued. "Do you want to make this your life's work?"

Magnus and Ivar looked at each other, and their smiles faded. Ivar spoke first. "I'm not worthy, Lars. I have not lived a godly life."

"Why would they want us? We're sinners," Magnus added.

"Do you remember going to church as children?" Lars asked.

"Yes," Magnus responded.

"Did you sing, pray, and read the Bible?" Lars probed further.

"Yes," Ivar replied. "I remember a story about a boy who hit a mean giant with a stone from his sling, and the giant fell down."

"That boy was David," Lars shared. "God picked him to be a king. David had everything he could want, but he sinned. David was blinded to his wrongdoing until the Lord's prophet pointed out the sin."

"What did David do?" asked Ivar.

"He repented to God," Lars answered.

"Did God forgive him?" Magnus asked.

"Not only did God forgive him, God chose David's bloodline as the family for Jesus." Lars stopped talking and waited for the twins' reaction.

Magnus and Ivar locked eyes and nodded to each other. "Lars," Ivar began. "We want to repent to God right now."

"Here, in the inn?" Lars asked with a wide-eyed look.

"Our wrongdoing was out in the open, so our repentance should be too," Magnus declared.

D Marie

As Lars began the prayer, Ivar and Manus confessed their sins to the Lord. The other patrons stopped and stared in quiet awe. The innkeeper fell to his knees and asked the Lord for forgiveness of his callous behavior during the contest. The twins' prayer for forgiveness became their first witness to give God glory.

When the prayer was over, Magnus and Ivar looked at each other again and nodded. "Reverend Lars," Magus began, "would you ask that question again about our life's work?"

Lars smiled as he tried to hold back the tears in his eyes, "Do you want to make this your life's work? The courses will take four to five years. You'll have to catch up with the others prior to the formal, university training."

"Yes, Lars!" the twins agreed simultaneously.

"It is expensive." Lars continued.

"We have coins," Magnus shared.

"We have been saving for our future for many years," Ivar added.

"Splendid!" Lars gladly replied trying to control his emotions. "I taught at this university before I came here. I'll write a letter of introduction for you. It will be ready after you have seen your brother, Johann."

"Our brother, Johann," the twins acknowledged. "May God heal these wounds."

Chapter 34

The Restoration

Magnus and Ivar summoned their mental strength as they approached the royal palace. Their voices remained silent while images of seeing Johann filled their minds. An antagonizing feeling wanted them to turn back, but they marched on.

When Magnus and Ivar approached the palace gate, the guards bowed and escorted them in. The brothers gave each other a puzzled look as neither one of them had introduced themselves to the guards.

Is this the common practice? Magnus and Ivar wondered as they looked at each other and followed another set of guards inside the doorway.

The guards escorted them to the garden. When they saw Johann, he stood alone next to a large flower bed. The same area he had toiled over many years ago. Johann turned around and saw his brothers. He ran toward them, gathered his arms around them, and hugged Magnus and Ivar dearly. The guards backed away and let the brothers have their private time.

All three brothers wept. As they embraced, Magnus and Ivar felt the love Johann had for them. Johann could feel his brothers' remorsefulness and their love in return. It was a moment none of them wanted to end.

"Johann, I mean, Sire, we…" Magnus started to say and knelt to his knee. Ivar quickly did the same. "I am sorry for how I treated you."

"I do not deserve anything from you," Ivar added, "but please forgive me."

"Johann, I am not worthy to have you as a brother," Magnus continued, "but please forgive me."

Johann offered his hands and raised both of his brothers back to their feet. His eyes roamed back and forth slowly surveying their faces.

"I have prayed for this day ever since I was a little boy," Johann shared. "Grandma taught me to always keep love in my heart. Today, that prayer has been answered. Magnus, Ivar, you have always been forgiven. I forgave you before, and I forgive you now. You are my brothers, my family. I have always loved you. Please stay with me and my family here."

"We are not worthy, Johann," Ivar replied. "When we told father of our sorrow and wanting your forgiveness, he was not understanding."

Journey to the Glass Hill

"We now want to help others as you have always done," added Magnus. "We are beginning our journey to become ministers."

"The Lord provides!" Johann exclaimed.

"Provides what?" Magnus asked.

"As you were coming into the garden, I was praying," Johann shared. "Tea and I want to wait a while before we marry. I prayed about who will be here after Reverend Lars retires. Tea and I would be honored if you two would perform our marriage ceremony when you return." Magnus and Ivar were speechless as Johann continued. "You have an inheritance coming, my brothers. Grandma's cottage is yours. It's been blessed by Reverend Gudmund. It's very fitting to have family and ministers of the Lord living there again."

Magnus and Ivar took a deep breath. When they exhaled, they felt a tremendous heaviness lift off their bodies. Johann blessed them even though they didn't deserve it. All they had to do was receive it. For the first time, they felt the meaning of true inner peace. They were truly and totally forgiven.

"Johann, I have something of yours," Magnus shared. "I wanted to give it to you many times, but I was afraid."

"Afraid of me?"

"No, afraid of our father. If he saw it, he might take it away from you." Ivar gave his brother a puzzled look. "I kept it a secret from Ivar, too." Magnus reached into his pocket and pulled out a toy horse, the one Ari had carved for Johann many years ago, and handed it to Johann.

Johann marveled at the little horse. "I remember this toy. Thank you, Magnus. Let's have a contest. First one of us that has a son, gets the toy horse."

"Unfair! You're betrothed. We don't have time for that. We'll be studying," Ivar said with a slight smile.

"It's fair. Remember, I'm waiting for your return," Johann said. "You two will be great fathers."

D Marie

The three brothers said their final goodbyes. Magnus and Ivar went back to the inn and gathered their belongings and horses. They walked their horses over to the church where Lars waited with their letter of introduction.

"God be with you, Magnus and Ivar," said Lars as he blessed them. "You know, I am retiring in a couple of years, and this town is growing so large that we will need two ministers to take care of the flock of Christana."

Magnus and Ivar both looked at Lars, then at each other. That confirmed what Johann had told them. They simultaneously said, "The Lord provides! Thank you, Reverend Lars!"

"I think I will be needing a new horse," Lars shared as he winked at them. "Tomorrow, I will ask your father if he has a gentle horse for an old man such as myself. It will give me an opportunity to keep Ari up-to-date with the news in Christana."

"Please tell him we will be living in Grandma's cottage when we return. It is a gift from Johann," Magnus said with a joyful heart.

"Johann wants the new ministers to live in the cottage and perform his marriage ceremony with Princess Tea," Ivar added.

"Splendid! Peace be with you Magnus and Ivar, and God bless you both. I have a gift for you, a Bible. You have a new journey ahead of you. Keep your eyes on Jesus for He will guide your paths."

Magnus and Ivar started to argue about who gets to ride with the Bible first. They looked up at Lars who stood on the church's steps frowning. Magnus offered to let Ivar carry the Bible first. Lars nodded and smiled. Magnus and Ivar waved goodbye. The brothers headed south and started their new journey.

Ari had watched, with tears in his eyes, as Magnus and Ivar rode their horses down the lane. He watched his sons until the

Journey to the Glass Hill

lane turned and they were out of view. Now, he was alone, totally alone, no Johanna, no sons, no family. With his head lowered, Ari forced his feet to walk into the house.

On the table, Ari noticed an unfamiliar book. "Whose book is this?"

The frayed edges of the cover and the yellowed pages indicated the Bible was old and well read. He sat down at the table and began to read.

I wonder if Johann could read and understand any of this? Is this what stirred up Magnus and Ivar this morning? Ari continued to read.

When you believe and pray to God, there is always hope.

Genesis 22:14 – Jehovah Jireh, The Lord will provide.

The journey continues with Part Two of the trilogy:

Journey to the Noble Horse

Chapters   *Discussion Starters*

1. If the wind is a type of metaphor, what Biblical representation comes to mind?

2. How can prayer help Elias?

3. Why would Elias be upset with busybodies?

4. What emotions is Ari feeling?

5. Why did the king invite the citizens of Christana to the wedding reception?

6. Why did the man in the pew nod his head?

7. What is a blessing?

8. What does "the Lord provides" mean?

9. Why doesn't Ari pray?

10. In what way was the king repaid for lending the services of the Court Physician and why was it as valuable as money?

11. What is the purpose of baptism?

12. Describe the differences between Elina's and Ari's relationship with God.

13. What could help Ari with his feelings toward Johann?

14. How can making mistakes help us?

15. Why did Elina want Johann to remember "the Lord provides"?

16. How did prayer give Johann his inner strength?

17. What could have prompted Magnus to question his father about Johann?

18. Describe the differences between Ari and Johann's way of dealing with the loss of a loved one.

19. How can new responsibilities help Johann?

20. How can the Bible impact Johann's life?

21. How does the Holy Spirit comfort someone?

22. Which characters had to be patient? Describe how they demonstrated patience.

23. What are some examples of Johann's spiritual growth?

24. What missed opportunity did Ari have with Reverend Lars?

25. How can Johann's memorable event affect his character?

26. What is trust?

Journey to the Glass Hill

27. How does the phrase, "the Lord provides" affect Johann?

28. Compare Johann's attitude to the contest to his brother's attitudes.

29. Describe the attitudes of the suitors.

30. How did Johann ward off negative feelings?

31. How did the Lord use Johann for His provision?

32. What characteristics did King Albert look for in his search for his future king and son-by-marriage?

33. Describe what happened to Magnus and Ivar after they read the Bible.

34. What did Magnus and Ivar receive from Johann? How did they feel afterward?

What will happen to Ari in the next book?

Acknowledgements

Journey to the Glass Hill has been an adventure for this novice author. Teaching a child to read a book is easy but writing a book required skills that I did not obtain in my university training. There was a strong desire inside of me to retell the *Princess on the Glass Hill* folktale from a Christian prospective. I knew the beginning and the end, but the in between chapters were all created with the help of the Creator.

Beyond offering wholesome entertainment for the reader, this book is designed to be a learning tool. During the course of writing this book, I lost five immediate family members. Their passing had a profound effect on the personal responses of the characters dealing with grief. My allowing the Lord to provide His comfort, made the message of this book, "the Lord provides," impact my life, too.

I am grateful for the helpful advice from many readers. Glenda Jameson initially edited my work. I had many mistakes. My beta-readers, Susan Marshall, Rosie Adle, Kathy Maske, Lucy Robertson, and Karen Mara each added valuable insight to enhance the story.

The illustrations in each of the chapters are the gifted handiwork of Reverend Brian King. He gave a visual representation of the characters and artifacts in the story. Deborah Jayarathne crafted the cover of the book displaying the young man, Johann. I am most appreciative of their talents and patience of getting the images just right.

Greg Baker, my editor, bless his heart, had to "take me to school" and guide me in writing techniques. He went above and beyond his role as an editor. Without him, my book would have suffered.

D Marie

My husband, Walter, listened to rough drafts and watched numerous writes and rewrites. His patience and support helped me to persevere to finish the journey.

About the Author

D Marie has taught school for over thirty years. She incorporated various educational methods to develop the joy of reading. D Marie designed this inspirational book as a learning tool to nurture Christian character and living. She is currently writing part two of the Journey trilogy, *Journey to the Noble Horse*. D Marie lives in the Midwest with her husband and family.

www.DMarieBooks.com

Artists

Illustrations: Brian King is the Pastor of Family Ministry at the Lutheran Church of Webster Gardens in St. Louis, Missouri.

Cover Design: Deborah Jayarathne

Journey to the Glass Hill is the story of one boy's endeavors through the trying times of his childhood. Johann, like most boys, just wanted to be loved, but with a father who was consumed with grief, he sought for this love to no avail. So, it was in other ways that Johann had to discover what love was. He found it in the animals around his father's farm and in the pages of an old Bible.

However, life is molded by more than circumstances. There were individuals who influenced Johann's journey and shaped his future. A kindly king, a gracious princess, a hungry beggar, and a heartbroken father all touched Johann's life in profound ways. But it was the absence of others that often weighed most intensely upon Johann's young shoulders—a mother and grandmother lost to him, and only fragmented memories remained to sustain him through the lows of life.

"The Lord will provide," became a mantra to him, an assurance his grandmother had often shared. And through the many trials that Johann faced, it was this truth that provided him with the strength to endure and develop into a young man of integrity with a kind and compassionate spirit. Eventually, his journey led to the slopes of the Grass Hill, and it was upon those slopes that he would discover if God could indeed provide and keep the promises Johann had discovered in that old Bible. It would be on those slippery slopes that God's will and plan would be made clear.

Made in the USA
Las Vegas, NV
18 January 2022